CORDELIA?
by Garson Kanin

"A REFRESHINGLY FINE PIECE OF FICTION..."
—Richmond Times Dispatch

"A SOPHISTICATED FROLIC THAT AMUSES..."
—Publishers Weekly

"DEFT AND UNPREDICTABLE..."
—The Atlantic Monthly

ZEBRA HAS IT ALL!

PAY THE PRICE   (1234, $3.95)
by Igor Cassini
Christina was every woman's envy and every man's dream. And she was compulsively driven to making it—to the top of the modeling world and to the most powerful peaks of success, where an empire was hers for the taking, if she was willing to PAY THE PRICE.

PLEASURE DOME   (1134, $3.75)
by Judith Liederman
Though she posed as the perfect society wife, Laina Eastman was harboring a clandestine love. And within an empire of boundless opulence, throughout the decades following World War II, Laina's love would meet the challenges of fate . . .

DEBORAH'S LEGACY   (1153, $3.75)
by Stephen Marlowe
Deborah was young and innocent. Benton was worldly and experienced. And while the world rumbled with the thunder of battle, together they rose on a whirlwind of passion—daring fate, fear and fury to keep them apart!

FOUR SISTERS   (1048, $3.75)
by James Fritzhand
From the ghettos of Moscow to the glamor and glitter of the Winter Palace, four elegant beauties are torn between love and sorrow, danger and desire—but will forever be bound together as FOUR SISTERS.

BYGONES   (1030, $3.75)
by Frank Wilkinson
Once the extraordinary Gwyneth set eyes on the handsome aristocrat Benjamin Whisten, she was determined to foster the illicit love affair that would shape three generations—and win a remarkable woman an unforgettable dynasty!

Available wherever paperbacks are sold, or order direct from the Publisher. Send cover price plus 50¢ per copy for mailing and handling to Zebra Books, 475 Park Avenue South, New York, N.Y. 10016. DO NOT SEND CASH.

BY GARSON KANIN

ZEBRA BOOKS
KENSINGTON PUBLISHING CORP.

ZEBRA BOOKS

are published by

KENSINGTON PUBLISHING CORP.
475 Park Avenue South
New York, N.Y. 10016

Copyright © 1982 by T.F.T. Corporation.
Reprinted by arrangement with Arbor House Publishing Company.

Quotation from *Private Lives*, © Noel Coward, 1930. Reprinted by permission of the Noel Coward Estate.

"The Lama" from *Verses from 1929 On* is reprinted by permission of Little, Brown and Company. © 1931 by Ogden Nash. First appeared in *The New Yorker*.

"On Children" from *The Prophet* is reprinted by permission of Alfred A. Knopf, Inc. © 1923 by Kahlil Gibran.

All rights reserved. No part of this book may be reproduced in any form or by any means without the prior written consent of the Publisher, excepting brief quotes used in reviews.

Printed in the United States of America

Cordelia?

One

I am going to write it down. I wonder if I can? I certainly am no writer, but then this is meant for no reader. Having played 49 parts in 46 plays in the course of my 28 years in the theater, I once tried to *write* a play. Somewhere in the wilds of Act Two I abandoned it. Awful. But this is different. I am doing it (trying to) at the instigation of the wisest man I know, the only sage I have ever encountered.

"Write it down," he said to me. "Write it all out. Thought, worry, anxiety, indecision—they're all abstract. But paper and pen and ink are concrete."

"I don't know if I can," I said.

"You can try, surely. Do you recall that delightful witticism of E. M. Forster's? He said, 'How can I tell what I think till I see what I say?'"

"Well, I suppose I can try."

"By all means."

That was more than three months ago. Why did I, on a sudden, nutty impulse that Sunday, fly out to Cincinnati to see Ben? Because I have known him for 23 years and recognize greatness when I see it. How did I first meet him, anyway?... Of course. Through the Lunts. I was playing with them in *The Visit* by Frederick Dürrenmatt. 1958. My first real Broadway break. And the show in which I met Pam, who was understudying in it.

I was standing in the wings one night just after places had been called, when Mr. Lunt came onstage and stood beside me.

"And how are *you* tonight, young man?" he asked.

"Fine," I replied hoarsely. I was astonished. Neither he nor Miss Fontanne ever spoke to anyone before a performance.

"I'm as nervous as a cat," he said, cracking his knuckles. "As nervous as a *nervous* cat."

"Why?"

"Ben Steinmetz's out front tonight."

"Who?"

"Dr. Benjamin Steinmetz. You've never heard of him?"

"No."

Mr. Lunt laughed. "Say, you haven't got much of a part here, have you? 'Why?' 'Who?' 'No.'"

"Yes," I said, and we both laughed.

"Ben Steinmetz," he said, "is the greatest man I know. A scientist, a writer, a super-intelligence, a fountain of wisdom and a monument of common

CORDELIA?

sense. Besides which, he knows more about the theater than anyone. Than *me*."

"Oh, I doubt that."

"What's more, he's a man with no guile of any kind. Says what he thinks, and what he thinks matters to me."

"I'd certainly love to meet him."

"Would you? Then come to supper with us. He's rather old, sixty-eight—I'm only sixty-*six,* you know—but he loves young people."

"Thank you, Mr. Lunt. I feel most privileged."

"You are. Say, what do you say to this? Dress quickly, come to my room, I'll introduce you and you can go on ahead with him. I hate to make him wait around while Lynnie takes off one makeup and puts on another. Why each one requires its own false eyelashes is beyond me. Yes, you two go on ahead. Julius will fix you a drink."

So it was that at 11:10 P.M. (curtain time was 8:30 in those days) on June 6, 1958 I met the remarkable Dr. Benjamin Steinmetz. An extremely diminutive man with the energy of a bee. Enthusiastic, voluble, funny, ineffably charming. (What is charm? I wish I knew.) He certainly did not *look* 68. More like *38*. Wait. Sixty-eight in 1958 would mean that he is now 91! But on the night of our recent meeting, *I* was the one who finally wore out at about 2:00 A.M. He seemed prepared to go on talking endlessly.

I remember that 1958 taxi ride with him indelibly. I was 25, but we became the same age almost at once. He told me things about my part that amazed me.

He suggested ways in which I could improve my performance. I accepted them and later used them all. He talked reverently about the Lunts. I was determined to make this man my friend and in time, through correspondence and meetings in Cincinnati and New York—and one in Paris—he became and remains my dearest and most valued friend.

Which is why I flew out to Cincinnati that Sunday to discuss my terrifying problem with him. It is more than a problem. It is an agonizing dilemma.

We went out to dinner at the antiquated German family restaurant he frequents, and talked of all sorts of things, among them, the amazing success of *King Lear* which I had then been playing for three weeks.

He said, "Oh, I knew it would be, fifteen minutes into that grand opening night. I'm *so* glad I was there."

I told him about the movie I made last spring, the plans for *next* year at Stratford. About the *Private Lives* tour—well, some of it, not all. And about Pam and the girls. He seemed especially interested in news of Cordelia, which, in view of the situation, troubled me greatly.

"What is it?" he asked. "Is *she* the problem? Or part of it?"

"Don't ask me that, Ben."

"Very well."

"Not yet, anyway. I'm madly confused. Crazy. I feel like I'm cracking up. Jesus! How can you tell when you're having a nervous breakdown?"

CORDELIA?

"There's no such thing," he said as he reached across the table, took my wrist and checked my pulse rate.

In spite of my agony, I laughed.

"What?" he asked.

"I'm wondering what all these staid people in here will make of this. Us holding hands."

"Calm down," he said, "and let's go. You're too agitated to eat."

I looked down at my plate full of tempting sauerbraten, potato pancakes and red cabbage. "Seems a wicked waste, Ben. All this good food."

"If you succumbed to a coronary occlusion," he said, "it would be a bigger waste."

We began walking back to his place at the Vernon Manor in silence. I was thinking and he was letting me.

About halfway there he said, "Have you ever told me why she's called Cordelia?"

"Of course."

"I've forgotten. Tell me again."

"It was during that Shakespeare summer in sixty-one. She was conceived after the opening performance of *Lear*."

"Ah, yes, now I remember. Your first *Lear*. *That* was a mistake, wasn't it?"

"Monumental."

"But no matter, really. When you have a failure, you must say to yourself, 'Well, *this* one didn't go.' That's all. No more, no less. So that particular *Lear* didn't and this one did."

"I had to do it again, Ben. A challenge. And *anything* to wipe out the memory of that horrible nineteen sixty-one misbegotten adventure."

"The first time, you played him too old," said Ben. "A common young person's fault."

I smiled and said, "How right you are! Once, at the Academy, I was playing Chris Christopherson in *Anna Christie*. I was nineteen. Mr. Jehlinger shouted at me from the auditorium, 'How old is this man, Standish—do you know?' And I said, 'Of course I know, sir. He's fifty-six.' 'Fifty-six! Good. If he were as old as *you're* playing him, he'd be dead!' Then he told me to go out and run around the block three times and when I came back, he asked, 'How do you feel?' And I said, 'All right, but a little tired right now.' 'Well,' he said, 'that's what a fifty-six-year-old man feels like *all* the time.'"

Ben laughed. "Lear has three young daughters and you played him dodderingly with a beard down to his navel. And they loaded you with those feckless effects. Offstage thunder and onstage lightning.

> *Blow, winds, and crack your cheeks. Rage, blow!*
> *You cataracts and hurricanoes, spout*
> *Till you have drenched our steeples, drowned the cocks.*

The thunder and lightning and winds have to be in the *words*. In the *poetry*."

"Thanks, Ben. The effects were out this time

because I told Peter what you'd said in sixty-one and he said you were just damn right."

"Does she like her name?"

"Who? Cordy?"

"Cordelia."

"We call her Cordy."

"Because she doesn't like Cordelia?"

At that moment, as he asked that question, I knew I would not be able to tell him about the frightful situation and what living alone with it was doing to me. I would probably never be able to tell *anyone*. I would have to make the decision by myself. When we got to his rooms, he made a pot of herbal tea, ritually, and served it.

"Now, then," he said.

"Ben, I'm miserably sorry and I apologize for taking up all this time, but I don't think I can ask you what I came to ask you." He said nothing, sipped his tea. "It's simply too personal. I thought I'd be . . . but no. I'm no damned good at . . . I mean, I get embarrassed to a point and . . . I suppose that's why I never went in for psychoanalysis. I couldn't possibly lie there and . . ." I had run out of words.

After a pause, he asked, "Is there more than one principle involved?"

"No."

"More than one other person?"

"Oh, yes."

"I see. Could you talk *around* it? Without details?"

"Maybe. I don't know." I got up and walked

about. Finally I asked him, "Are there times when the truth ought to be buried?"

"Certainly."

"When?"

"Many times. For instance, when the truth might prove to be damaging to innocent people. And in any case, truth is ephemeral. My truth. Your truth. His truth. That old chestnut: 'There are three sides to every story—yours, his and the truth.' Some think that the truth is whatever you believe."

"Sorry, that's beyond me."

"And me. But let me give you an example. Got a minute? Some years ago there was a distinguished justice of the Ohio State Supreme Court. A truly fine man, greatly beloved and respected. Wife, children, grandchildren. Before his appointment to the bench, he was here at the university, in the law school, and we were friends. I saw him often, a superlative man—interested in *everything*. Goethe and baseball and nutrition and jazz music. He came to me once and asked me, as a physiologist, if I thought the waning of sexual power and capability was inevitable. I told him that I did *not* think so, that it was largely a matter of the mind, and that a healthy man could expect to be a lover until the day of his death, if he could find the magic of a stimulating partner. As it happened, this proved to be only too prophetic. A short time after our talk, he engaged a new secretary. His old one had retired. The new young woman was bright and beautiful. They fell—no, they *grew* in love. He was sixty-six, she was twenty-four. Late one afternoon, while making love at her cottage on the river he suffered a massive seizure and died. This exceptional young lady did not panic. She called her older brother, a doctor, who came to her at once. They discussed the situation calmly, pragmatically, and finally agreed upon a course of action. Together, they dressed the justice's body, waited until dark, then carried the body out to his car. The brother drove, his sister followed in *her* car. A few blocks from the justice's home, the brother ditched the car, posed the body behind the wheel and left it. By this time, an alarm had gone out for the missing justice, and so, before long, his car was found. It seemed clear to everyone that he had had a heart attack while driving home. There followed a most impressive funeral, condolences from hundreds, including President Eisenhower. However. A man, a neighbor of the young woman, something of a voyeur, had observed the happening and a few days later anonymously telephoned the justice's wife and told her the whole story. She had, it turned out, harbored some suspicion about the judge and his secretary for some time past. Now, in a violent fit of recrimination, she went to the authorities with the information. They apprehended the young woman and her brother. When faced with the accusation, easily provable, what with fingerprints and so on, they confessed. Charges were brought—more serious against the brother than against the young woman. He was a doctor, after all, who had failed to report a death—worse, had concealed it. He was sent to prison for some months, I forget how many. Later he was expelled from the medical association, license revoked, left Cincinnati. I've no idea as to where he is or what's become of him. His sister—after a manslaughter charge was dropped—went to Europe. She came to see me before she left and told me she was never coming back. And as far as I know, she never has. The plans to erect a statue of the justice in Piat Park were quietly dropped. People seldom mentioned his name, except in vulgar, sniggering jest. This splendid man. What was his crime, really? The exercise of as natural a function as there is in the whole spectrum of human behavior. So there you have it. What did the exposure of the truth in *that* case accomplish? The wreckage of several lives and the bringing of pain to others and the besmirchment of a glorious reputation. Truth!"

I said nothing but thought about the story for a long time, wondering how it applied to *my* quandary.

"There's nothing criminal about mine, Ben. And for all I know the revelation of the truth in *my* case might bring joy to some or maybe even . . . I don't know."

"And if it were to be left alone?" he asked.

"Well, in that case," I said, "probably the only one who'd be damaged would be me."

"In what way?"

"*Living* with it, Ben. Living with it, as I've been doing for months. Uncertain. Ambivalent. One day I think this, another night I'm sure of the opposite."

"It would help if I knew more."

"I know, but I can't—not now, anyway. May I use the bathroom?"

"That's what it's for," he said.

When I returned I noticed that it was almost 2:00 A.M. I apologized.

"No need," he said. "I've been thinking. Write it down. Write it all out. For yourself."

Two

So. I begin. At the very beginning.

The summer of 1961. Pam and I were playing the Shakespeare season at Stratford, Ontario, Canada. Each of us had—with rare good fortune—scored solidly in separate plays on Broadway the year before, and had suddenly become "names." Like many theater couples, we were all at once infected with a serious case of Luntitis: the dream of emulating them and becoming the theatrical couple of *our* generation. So when the dual offer from Stratford came, we jumped at it. We did *As You Like It* (a hit, mainly due to Pam's entrancing Rosalind); *Macbeth* (a small mistake; we both gave overwrought performances—partly the fault of the overwrought director); and *King Lear* (a shattering lapse of judgment). At the age of 28 I had no business taking so wild a leap of faith. I had heard that Scofield and Olivier and Kean had all done it before 30—but those guys were better trained. (And better actors?) And Orson here, but, hell, he can do anything.

We were in the habit of staying up late after the show each night, partly to wind down and have supper, but mainly to rehash the performance and look for improvements. Alfred Lunt had once said to *The Visit* company after a show, "Nothing matters, nothing, except the quality of the performance we gave tonight."

One night, after a *Lear* during which I was drenched with flop-sweat, we ate (not enough) and drank (too much) and were less garrulous than usual. No wonder. What was there to say? Later, in our rented house we took a second shower together and began to get ready for bed. Pam was brushing her hair. In the soft, dim light, I was admiring her nakedness. I had never gotten used to it. Hell, I'm not used to it *now*. It is the most beautiful body I have ever seen and it always makes me wish I were a painter or a sculptor so that I might try to immortalize it.

She turned and regarded me.

"Whaddaya lookin' at, Buster?" she asked in her gun-moll voice.

"Mine," I replied.

We started for the bed—we slept in the nude that hot summer—but instead of piling in as we usually did, we held one another's eyes. My heartbeat quickened. I knew what was coming, I swear it.

"Would you care to hear something interesting?" she asked.

"You're pregnant," I said.

"Why don't you just say 'Yes'? Stop padding your part. Now, I'll give you your cue again. . . . Would you care to hear something interesting?"

"Yes."

"I'm pregnant," she said.

After a long, frozen minute I moved to her and we embraced gently.

"I knew it before you said it."

"How?"

"That look, that expression. I've only seen it twice before—once when you announced Lynn and again when it was going to be what turned out to be Laurette."

We kissed, then got into bed and clung to one another.

"This one," she said, "is going to be Cordelia."

"A *boy* named *Cordelia?*" I asked.

"It's a girl."

"How do you know?"

"Because I want it to be."

"All right. Cordelia she is. And remember, it's back to listening to all that Mozart. Nine months of Mozart."

(Our friend Thornton Wilder, when we played *Our Town* in Williamstown had said that pregnant women should listen to Mozart . . . "Because it's the sound most harmonious to the life and spirit of human beings and the burgeoning fetus is calmed and soothed and affected through the mother's subliminal reaction." That was good enough for us, and Pam did it religiously both times.)

Pam said, "With the aid of my trusty little adding machine *and* my diary *and* my feminine whatnot, I happen to know for certain exactly when she was conceived."

"When?"

"Opening night of *Lear*."

"Are you sure? I thought we were too..."

"We were not too... and we did. Beautifully. That's why Cordelia."

We slept soundly.

The next morning was time for the practical considerations. The season still had seven weeks to run. What about all the necessary prenatal care? How long should Pam continue to play? What about all that physical stuff in *Macbeth?* What about the Neil Simon play we were supposed to do in the fall? Would he wait? Did we have the right to ask him? Should I do it with someone else? More questions than answers. And what about telling the kids? Lynn was three; Laurette not yet two.

In the end, most of the questions answered themselves as they so frequently do. The girls were told and began to behave as though *they* were the parents of the expected baby. Boy or Girl became their new game.

CORDELIA?

Neil, a prince, said he *would* wait. We finished the Stratford season happily exhausted and went to Vermont for a month.

I got a movie job at Twentieth and we all went out to California for the duration of the picture. Thank God we were able to make it back east in time. Dr. Groh, the Beverly Hills obstetrician, had confirmed Pam's prediction of a girl and some wacky instinct in me objected to a Shakespearean child being born in Holmby Hills.

So it was that the Gotham Hospital for Women became the scene of Cordelia's birth. Our friend Dr. Fred Herter had recommended both the obstetrician and the pediatrician and Pam was calm and happy throughout.

I had not been present at the other two births but Dr. Levin, young and progressive, suggested that I attend this one. I did not enjoy it.

When it was over I phoned the children. Each of them picked up an extension. "Well, kids," I said, "you have a baby sister."

"Is it a boy or a girl?" asked Laurette.

Great times followed. We were a family, complete.

Lynnie continued to grow ever more graceful and willowy. She danced. And sang. She imitated everyone and everything. She began to take ballet lessons and was soon the star of her class.

Laurette, too, seemed to have been born to the

boards. At The Dalton School, at the age of eight, she played Lady Macbeth. I shall not exaggerate and say that she was good but as Pam said, "Let's face it. She was every bit as good as *I* was in the part in sixty-one."

Cordelia, as time passed, turned out to be the quiet one. Shy, introverted and thoughtful.

One summer in Easthampton, Lynnie discovered The Game—that modern form of charades. She was especially good at it and insisted on organizing sessions whenever the opportunity presented itself.

At Laurette's tenth birthday party there was trouble.

As soon as Lynnie had begun to choose up sides for The Game, Cordelia had disappeared. Lynn was an aggressive, forceful child who had to have her own way, so Cordy's defection upset her. She sought Cordy and brought her, crying, to me.

"Tell her she's *got* to, Daddy!"

"Wait a second."

"I won't!" cried Cordelia. "I hate it! I won't! It's stupid."

"Well, look, Lynnie," I said, "if she doesn't *want* to—"

"She *never* wants to do *anything!* She'll ruin *everything.* We're an even number. If she won't play, somebody else is going to get left out. A guest!"

I turned to Cordelia. "Won't you help out, Cordy, just this once?"

CORDELIA?

She stopped crying and looked at me. Those eyes. Those blue blue eyes. I thought *I* was going to start crying.

She spoke in a near-whisper. "If you want me to, Daddy." Then she shouted, "But I *hate* it!"

"Good girl."

I went out with them to watch The Game.

Laurette's turn. She conveyed "Things go better with Coke" in three gestures. Six seconds. Yay!

On the opposing team a boy of eight had trouble with "Ask not what your country can do for you, ask what you can do for your country." His side managed the first part, but it took them four minutes to complete.

Then Cordelia drew: *"A Hard Day's Night."* I saw her struggle bravely, gamely, to no avail. She blushed, sweated, trembled. I reproached myself for having forced her into this ordeal. Time ran out. Groans.

The Game continued but I went out to the bar and poured myself a double.

"You asleep, love?" I whispered to Pam later that night.

"Mmm."

"I'm going to get some milk. You want some milk?"

"What time is it?"

"Three-forty."

"All right," she said wearily. "Milk."

"I'm going to stick some booze into mine. Join me?"

"My father's joke," she said. "Remember?"

"No," I replied, sliding out of bed.

"'Will you join me in a cup of tea?' 'Well, why don't you get in first and then if there's room, I will?'"

Glasses in hand, we settled down to talk.

"You know what beats me?" I asked.

"What?"

"Those kids. How different they are."

"From what?"

"From each other."

"Well, I should think so. Different ages. Teachers, influences, interests."

"You know what I mean, love. Here they are, same mother, same father—"

"You have my word on it. God! How much booze did you put into this?"

"One jigger."

"Scout's honor?"

"They get the same education, roughly. The same food, holidays, disciplines—follow?"

"Go on. Follow."

"And they're turning out all different."

"It's a free country," said Pam. "Isn't that the wonder of it? The greatness? Respect for the individual?"

"I'm not saying this well. Let me try again. What do you think Laurette is going to be?"

"President of the United States."

CORDELIA?

"Come on, Pam."

"All right, then. *Vice*-president. How the hell do *I* know?"

"Wait a second. Don't go back to sleep yet."

"I'm sleepy. And you're making me sleepier."

"God damn it! They're your kids, too. Don't you care what happens to them?"

"Not at four in the morning I don't."

"I see Laurette in the theater," I said. "But not as an actress finally. Or even a dancer."

"Why not?"

"She doesn't seem to have the let-go. No, her gift or aptitude or whatever you want to call it is more like . . . well, more running things, getting it all her way."

"So?"

"So that makes her a director. Or a choreographer. Potentially."

"You're a daffy, love. The girl's ten."

"When I was ten, I knew I was going to be an actor . . . even though my father was a master plumber and my mother was a contract bridge teacher. And what about *you* at ten?"

"At ten, I was madly and wetly in love with Marlon Brando because my drunken Uncle Albert had taken me to see *A Streetcar Named Desire* at the Ethel Barrymore Theater and—"

"There you are! Interested in the theater at—"

"Not at all. In sex."

"At ten?"

"At *nine!* I would dream—daydreams, that is—of

being kissed by Cary Grant."

"I thought you said Brando."

"Him, too. And Gary Cooper. And Fred Astaire."

"Jesus!"

"No, not him—but Errol Flynn. And Bing Crosby."

"Is that all?"

"For Mondays, yes."

"Proves my point. At ten you were an incipient sexpot and that's what you became."

"I see Laurette as a great woman of the theater. Director, actress, writer. A tough, female Noel Coward."

"And Lynn?"

"Well, not like the lady she was named for. Was that a mistake? Our Lynn will be the Shirley MacLaine of her time—a beauty who can sing and dance and act and be funny and never out of work."

"Cordelia?"

"A serious actress. Maybe *she* should have been named after Laurette Taylor. Listen, is it too late to switch names on them?"

"What makes you think 'actress' at all for Cordelia?"

"What else is there for anyone brought up around this zoo? She's the brainy one."

"Yes," I said. "Takes after me."

"Right. Conceited, egotistical, selfish."

"Now, now."

"Don't worry about Cordy. She's got it taped!"

"The thing we've got to look out for," I said, "is

CORDELIA?

forcing. We've got to remember to give them their heads. Don't you be a stage mother, and I promise not to be a stage father. Acting. It's a great life, but a tough one—especially for a girl—and more especially for an attractive one. Now we know about Lynn and Laurette, but I think Cordy's going to be a *great* beauty. I mean, not just a beauty in the accepted sense but a beauty inside and out—who doesn't trade on it. An intelligent, brilliant looker. Like Vivien Leigh. Is there anything more exciting? But still . . . she doesn't seem to have that sense of play that's absolutely essential to . . . what do *you* think? Pam? . . . Pam!"

"Yes," she said, "she *does* take after you."

We went back to sleep.

Three

Our personal Three Sisters grew and developed gloriously.

One Easter we bought them each a live white Easter rabbit. Big hit. We were living in Greenwich, Connecticut, at the time, and with the girls' help I built a small, wire-meshed rabbit hutch out in the garden. A grand week of observing and feeding (Lynnie's wouldn't eat carrots!) and watching the antics.

Laurette named her rabbit Spencer after her favorite actor, Spencer Tracy. Lynn's became Peter. And nothing could persuade Cordelia from calling hers simply Ears.

By the second week, only Cordy seemed interested, taking over the care of all three rabbits. One of them, Spencer, apparently tried to escape during a scary thunderstorm one night and tore its eye on a strand of the wire mesh.

Cordy went to pieces. I sent for Dr. Ives, the local vet, who examined Spencer while Cordy held him.

"Poor thing's a mess," he pronounced.

And indeed it was, with one seemingly dead eye hanging out of its sad head.

"Can you fix it?" asked Cordy anxiously.

"Well," said the doctor, "I doubt it. And anyway, what's the point? Takes time and money and you *have* got two others, haven't you?"

"Yes."

"Well, then—why not let me put this little fellow away?—out of his misery."

As he reached into his bag for a hypodermic needle, Cordelia screamed, more loudly than I would have thought possible from such a tiny throat, and still screaming, ran across the garden and into the house, clutching the wounded rabbit to her breast.

Dr. Ives, nonplussed, shrugged and said, "Well, when she's asleep tonight just give it one hard push with your thumbs under the front of its head—like this—and drop it into the incinerator."

I very nearly screamed myself.

Cordelia kept Spencer in her room for two weeks. She replaced the torn eye somehow, and kept bathing it with witch hazel, to which she was

CORDELIA?

inordinately attached, and bandaging it. She kept changing the bandage and applying whatever salves and lotions she could find in the house. She changed the rabbit's name from Spencer to Sore-eye. She went to the drugstore, asked Mr. Halloran, the pharmacist, for advice, and came home with boric acid, Collyrium, A & D ointment, and Neosporin ointment. She continued her ministrations, feeding and bathing Sore-eye with a dedication that was both comical and moving. The other two rabbits died—of neglect, I suppose—but Sore-eye thrived and in time recovered. He remained, until his death about a year later, a healthy and seemingly happy one-eyed rabbit.

A few months after the scene with Dr. Ives we had occasion to send for him to see Lynn's sick puppy, Shaggy. Cordelia wandered in holding Sore-eye and overacting nonchalance. When Dr. Ives failed to notice her she stepped in front of him.

"How are *you*, Cordy?" he asked.

"I'm fine," she replied, "and so's Sore-eye."

"Who?"

"This rabbit."

"Good."

"And *you* wanted to *kill* him!"

"Mind your manners, Cordy," I cautioned.

She looked at me, her eyes ablaze. *"He* wanted to *kill* him!"

Dr. Ives was amazed. "Is that the one? Really?"
"Really," I said.
"Let me see," he said, reaching out.
Cordelia said, "No!" resolutely and marched out of the room.
Dr. Ives tried a smile, failed, and said, "Well, we all make mistakes. Even rabbits."

Four

Was that the beginning of Cordelia and animals? Or did her involvement come even earlier without our noticing it? Or was it later when we bought her the filly for her thirteenth birthday? In any case, animals became and have remained a vital part of her life. There's hardly an important zoo in the country she hasn't visited. A few years ago, shortly after the publication of *All Creatures Great and Small* in the United States, Cordelia spent all her savings on a trip to Yorkshire to meet and pay her respects to the author, Dr. James Herriot. He is, to this day, her personal god.

And then there was the astonishing business of eyeglasses for Shaggy.

Frisbees became popular and instead of dogs chasing and returning sticks, they played with Frisbees. But poor Shaggy would miss it four times out of five, so the game became tedious for most of us. Not for Cordy. She was determined to teach Shaggy to catch the Frisbee and spent hours attempting to do so.

"You're wasting your time," said Laurette. "He just happens to be a dumb dog."

Cordy did not respond. She was deep in thought.

"It's *not* dumb," said Lynn. "It's a lack of coordination. That's why he bumps into furniture so much. It happens with people, too. Lack of coordination. If you don't have great coordination, you can't be a dancer, and it's only when coordination is sharpened and developed to a really high degree that you get to be any good."

"Reggie Jackson," I said aimlessly.

Cordy looked up. "When it's on his right side—Shaggy, I mean—he catches it just fine. It's the left side he always misses."

"Dogs are boring," announced Laurette.

"Nothing living is boring," said Cordy.

She spent a great deal of time with Shaggy, and one afternoon invited us all out into the yard to demonstrate his newfound skill.

Cordy had fashioned a pair of eyeglasses out of her underwater goggles, and had had the optometrist put a magnifier in the left lens.

Shaggy caught nine out of ten.

Later, Dr. Ives confirmed that Shaggy suffered

from astigmatism in his left eye. He wore his eyeglasses happily, caught Frisbees and squirrels and did not bump into furniture until we lost him one summer to a careless motorcycle gang.

During her last year at Dalton, discussions of Cordy's future began and continued sporadically. Pam and I were on tour and I admit were more interested in that than in what was happening back home. The girls would fly out—singly, in pairs, once all three—to see us, spend a Sunday, or make the next jump with us.

Laurette was in her third year at Juilliard and doing extremely well.

Lynn had joined the corps de ballet of The American Ballet Theatre, was working too hard, but showing great promise.

Cordelia caught up with us in Detroit over the Thanksgiving holiday.

Supper at the Pontchartrain.

"There's a zebra at the zoo here," said Cordelia, "that may be the most intelligent of his species I've ever seen."

"And how can you tell that, pray?" asked Pam.

"You judge a zebra's or anything's intelligence by observation," said Cordelia. "The way you can with people. How they move and eat and drink and react. I watched that zebra for two hours this afternoon and—"

"Two hours!" I said.

"—and the way it responded to the keeper who was feeding it was *phenomenal.*"

"You spent two hours watching a zebra?" I asked.

"What's wrong with that? You've spent two hours watching Emlyn Williams' *Charles Dickens* or even longer at a play or ballet. And what about that *eight* hours of *Nicholas Nickleby* in London?"

"The defense rests," I said.

"Where are we with plans?" asked Pam, getting down to business.

"It's really hard to decide," said Cordelia. "I really need some advice. Really."

"That's what we're here for," I said. "Really."

"No," said Cordelia. "I don't think so. I don't think you can help me."

"Why not?"

"Because look . . ." She reached into her capacious tote bag and pulled out what appeared to be three brochures. She handed two of them to me and one to Pam, who looked at it and winced. When I saw mine I understood why.

CATALOG
NEW YORK STATE
VETERINARY COLLEGE 1979-80
ITHACA, NEW YORK

UNIVERSITY OF WISCONSIN
VETERINARY SCHOOL
MADISON, WISCONSIN

Pam handed me hers. Texas. I offered mine. She shook her head.

CORDELIA?

It took me a minute to frame my next question. It came out inaudibly.

"What?" asked Cordelia and Pam in unison, and laughed.

"What *projection!*" said Pam.

"This may be the greatest Caesar salad in America," said Cordelia. "Have you got the clout to get me the recipe?"

Have I mentioned that she had become a vegetarian? And a damned nuisance it was, too. Especially on planes or trains or in restaurants. She had taken to carrying around a lunch box filled with her own special foods. Bulgar, tofu, bee pollen, oil of evening primrose.

I tried my question again. "What about Juilliard?"

"No," she said flatly.

"Not even for a year? Just to see?"

"What's to see?"

"You might like it."

"How could I? *Miss Laurette* likes it."

She and Laurette had had a falling out. We had hoped that it would be patched up in time, but no. Not so far.

"I'd always hoped," I said, "in fact, I *still* hope that we'd be a real theater family."

"What's so great about *that,* for God's sake!" she cried. "It's inbreeding. Like incestuous. Same same same."

I could see that Pam was even more upset than I but was struggling to remain calm.

"I thought we all agreed," she began in a shaky

voice, "that you'd try Juilliard for a year and then—"

"I changed my mind. I'm going to try Wisconsin for a year. Or Cornell. Or Baylor."

I took her hand and looked into her lovely blue blue eyes.

"Cordelia, love, I think you're far too beautiful to be a vetenarian. The animals won't appreciate you."

She pulled her hand away from mine. "To be a *what? What* did you say?"

"Did I get it wrong? Isn't that the plan? Vetenarian?"

Her celebrated temper surfaced. "You can't even *say* it, for Christ's sake! So how can you not want me to *be* it?"

"Cool it, Cordy," said Pam, looking around the room.

Cordelia's quietness as she continued served only to intensify her fury. "Veterinarian," she said through clenched teeth. "Not 'vetenarian.' *Jesus!*"

"Cordy!" said Pam.

"Well, I'll be damned," I said. "I never knew that."

"Probably because you never played one," said Pam.

That night, while Pam slept, I lay awake and thought of my father for the first time in years. I heard his rough, grating voice only too clearly: "An *actor* f'Chrissake! What *are* you? Some kind of a sissy? Want to paint your face? Well, hell, I might

CORDELIA?

have known it. You've always been a goddam showoff—peacock. So go on—try it. And after you've gone on your ass, come back and I'll teach you an *honest* trade. A *man's* trade. An' you *will* be back—mark my words."

He never saw me on the stage—not even after I had made several hits and was doing well. Since his death eight years ago—pneumonia—my mother comes to see every play I do. Often three or four times. Good or bad, she always loves them and me in them.

Was I behaving with Cordelia as my father had with me? To what extent should *any* parent attempt to control the destiny of a child?

Then, strangely, lines from *The Prophet* by Kahlil Gibran began floating through my mind.

Long, long ago, while I was still at the Academy, I had memorized it—on a bet—in two days, winning handily.

Your children are not your children.
They are the sons and daughters of Life's longing for itself.
Something something *through you but not from you,*
Something something *with you yet they do not belong to you.*
. . . your love but not your thoughts.
Their souls live in the house of tomorrow.
Something *try to be like them but seek not to make them like you.*

Something *life does not go backward nor does it tarry with yesterday.*
You are only the bows from which your children are set forth as living arrows.

"Leave her alone!" I heard myself say aloud.
"What?" asked Pam, half asleep.
"Nothing, love, nothing."
And before long, I slept peacefully.

Five

Late the following spring we were preparing to go back to Stratford, Ontario to play a summer season of *The Importance of Being Earnest* and *The Taming of the Shrew*.

Laurette was already on tour of European theaters. Lynn was getting ready to begin rehearsals with The American Ballet Theatre in New York.

A Sunday morning. First Lynn, then Cordelia piled into bed with us as they frequently did. Breakfast was catch as catch can.

"One thing about dancing," said Lynn, "you *hurt* all the time. I mean *all* dancers do. They should've told me."

"What if they had?" asked Cordelia.

"Oh, I'd've done it anyway, but at least I'd've known."

"I hate pain," said Cordelia.

Pam nudged me. My cue.

"Cordy . . ." I began tentatively.

"No!" she said.

We all laughed.

"All I was going to ask," I said, "is that I hope for God's sake—and ours—you won't change your mind about going to Baylor University in Texas in the fall to become a v-e-t-e-r-i-n-a-r-i-a-n. It would break my heart if you did."

"You kill me," said Cordy. "You really do. Why don't you get off this legit kick and be a stand-up comic?"

"I'll take it under advisement," I said.

"What you were *going* to say, *mon vieux,* was more like—" (here she found a baritone voice and began a disturbing, uncanny imitation of me, including characteristic gestures and mannerisms): "'Listen, Cordy, dear, you know how much we love you and have only your best interests at heart and your plans are *so* depressing that they keep us from sleeping—and besides, when people ask what you're doing and we have to tell them—it's simply blush-making time. But anyway, we're going to see you through and we know that you're going to be the best little *vetenarian* in the whole wide world, but—'"

"All right, Cordy, that's enough," said Pam, who could see my embarrassment.

Cordy, undeterred, plunged on. "'—but just for the fun of it, just for the hell of it, why don't you stick

CORDELIA?

with us this summer? And maybe, I don't know, maybe just as a lark—you could be in the plays with us. You could do Cecily in *Earnest* and Bianca in *Shrew* and we'd all have a real fun summer.'" She returned to her own voice and persona. *"That's* what you were going to say, wasn't it?"

I was speechless, covered with gooseflesh. It was indeed what I had planned to say—down to the two parts. How had she divined it? What sort of a supernatural sprite had I sired?

She giggled at my obvious discomposure.

"You're a witch," I said.

"Your idea being," she said, "that I would somehow get sucked in, bitten by the bug, become hopelessly stagestruck and forget all about Texas and that mundane nonsense—like the well-being of living creatures. So just to prove the point once and for all—here's the deal. *Yes!* Did you hear me? I said, yes. I'll stay. I'll do it. But not Cecily, she's too silly. I'll do Gwendolen. Beautifully. Bianca. O.K. A bore—but I'll do something with her." She stood up in bed, moved to the foot of it, placed a folded napkin on her head to simulate a bonnet and in a faultless and beguiling British accent began to speak as Gwendolen:

Ernest, we may never be married. From the expression on Mamma's face, I fear we never shall. Few parents nowadays pay any regard to what their children say to them. The old-fashioned respect for the young is fast dying out. Whatever influence I ever had over Mamma, I lost at the age of three. But although she may prevent us from becoming man and wife, and I may marry someone else and marry often, nothing that she can possibly do can alter my eternal devotion to you.

She jumped down from the bed and began taking a series of vaudeville-style bows, running in and out of the room. Pam and Lynn were applauding enthusiastically. Then Lynn added that piercing finger-whistle she had picked up somewhere and which she had promised me *never* to use indoors. For my part, I found that I was not applauding. Why not? I couldn't. Letter-perfect though Cordy had been, and spirited though her reading, I suspected that she would fail to make contact with the audience. I had seen too many good performances remain on stage and never cross the footlights.

Cordy noted my reservation almost at once. "No good?" she asked.

"Astonishing," I said.

"That can mean anything," she said.

"How come you memorized that speech?" I asked.

"I know the whole part," she replied. "In fact, the whole play. Would you care to hear some Algernon?"

"Not right now."

"Well, was that wrong to do? To learn it? Isn't that what you and Mom do?"

"You bet."

"So?"

"So nothing. I'm just surprised."

"But not delighted."

"When's the last time I spanked you, missy?"

"Nineteen seventy-five," she said. "And it didn't hurt a bit."

"It will next time," I said. "I've been practicing."

"On whom, may I ask?"

I should have known better than to tangle with her.

Six

Rehearsals began. Cordelia impressed everyone on the first day. She was lively, sure-footed and charming. And, even *I* had to admit, good.

But in the week that followed my misgivings about her began to surface again. What the hell was it? What was bothering me? Was it self-consciousness about the fact that she was my daughter? If so, why had I never felt it about Laurette or Lynn?

Toward the end of the second week I began to see what the trouble was although no one else—not even Pam—did. Cordelia was simply not growing or ripening or progressing in the part. She was good on the first day and good on the eleventh. No better, no worse. She had thought out a performance, and that was that.

I have found that in acting there is no such thing as a frozen performance—that is for films. In the theater there is constant fluctuation and if you're not getting better you're getting worse.

I longed to talk to her, to work with her, to coach her, but I feared that creating any difficulty whatever might upset my whole scheme—the one she had perceived so eerily.

Of course I had hoped that a summer of playing with a first-class company, sharing the excitements and joys of communal creation, coming to sense the warm camaraderie and enjoying the applause would indeed lure her away from the prospect of dealing for the rest of her life with sick animals. But whenever the subject came up, however subtly, she would tease me mercilessly.

"Oh, Dad!" she cried one day at a picnic lunch on the lawn. "What fun this is! What a fool I've been! All I want to do in life from now on is act! Act! Act!"

Another time: "Honestly, Dad! The way you keep watching me for a sign. Will you know when it comes? Do I break into a stage-struck rash? Does a spotlight from nowhere hit me?"

She was winning every round. And then. And then something happened that neither Pam nor I had anticipated although we should have. Fate. Fortune. Destiny. Karma. Appointment in Samarra—or Stratford.

There was an excellent actor in the company named Timothy Wakeman. He had been with us in the Bob Anderson play and we had suggested him to the people here to play Algernon in *Earnest* and Christopher Sly in *Shrew*. He had it all—looks, power, instinct, humor, masculinity, experience, intelligence and magnetism. We were convinced that he would go far. We got to talking about him at breakfast one morning, about how completely different he was in his two parts and about his certain great future.

"I doubt it," said Cordelia with her mouth full of waffle.

"Are you in a position to make that judgment?" I snapped. She irritated the hell out of me sometimes. "With your vast professional theatrical experience?"

"Oh, don't get testy, ol' boy, not at breakfast. It's just an opinion—not even that—conversation. Who cares?"

Pam spoke gently. "But I'm interested, Cordy. What do you think is wrong with him?"

"He's too *manny*. That's what. Sort of a peacock. I think he's in love with himself."

Not long afterward, following a late rehearsal, a few of us went to a diner down the road for supper. It was crowded and we found ourselves sharing a booth with Cordelia and Tim.

The plump, sexy waitress appeared and managed to take all four orders without once taking her eyes off of Tim.

Pam said, "I'll have a chef's salad and iced coffee, please."

"Cordy?"

"Go ahead. I'm still thinking."

I ordered. "Club sandwich on rye. Bacon crisp? Jack Daniel's soda."

Tim looked at Cordy, who shrugged. He said, "Cheeseburger medium. Ale. Molson's if you have it."

"Oh, sure," said the waitress with love.

"All right, same for me," said Cordy.

I sensed Pam tremble beside me and I suppose she was aware of *my* physical reaction. To our knowledge, Cordy had not eaten meat in four years or had had ale ever. But we wisely kept our silence.

"Mind if I smoke?" asked Tim.

"No," said Pam, "but *you* do."

He laughed lightly and lit a cigarette.

"Well, Tim," I said, "we haven't had much of a chance to chat what with this and that. What do you make of it all?"

"I think I'm in love with Oscar Wilde," he said.

"I hope not," said Cordy. "He's a bugger."

"Was," said Tim. "Anyway, does it matter? What a play he gave us! Has English ever tasted more delicious?"

We talked about *Earnest* until the food arrived, then switched to *Shrew*.

"It's really pretty raunchy," said Cordy. "Are you going to leave all that rough stuff in?"

"What rough stuff?"

She looked at Tim and quoted:

CORDELIA?

If I be waspish, best beware my sting.

Tim picked up the cue and they played out the scene—badly, I was pleased to note.

TIM *(as Petruchio)*
My remedy is then to pluck it out.

CORDY *(as Katharine)*
Aye, if the fool could find out where it lies.

TIM
Who knows not where a wasp does wear his sting? In his tail.

CORDY
In his tongue.

TIM
Whose tongue?

CORDY
Yours, if you talk of tails, and so farewell.

TIM
What, with my tongue in your tail?

Cordy looked at me and said, "*That* rough stuff."
"Really, Tim!" said Pam, truly shocked.
It had been years since I had seen her blush.
"Don't blame me, Pam," he said. "Blame the Bard."
"I guess this production'll be X-rated, huh?" said Cordy. "Even so, don't be surprised when a few of

the blue-haired ladies walk out. There may be quite a parade. Quite a."

"Don't worry," I said. "I've got a way of handling all that."

"What is it?" asked Tim.

"I mug and slur the words so they know I've said something smutty but they don't know what."

"Clev-*er!*" said Tim, tapping his temple.

"I've noticed that, you faker!" cried Cordy. "I thought you were up or something."

"No, no, just:

What? With my gung in your mail?"

Tim and Cordy howled. I went on. "When Alfred Lunt played it, he didn't say the words at all. He conveyed it all with two brilliant gestures:

What? With my [gesture] in your [gesture]?"

"Terrific," said Tim. "Why don't *you* do that?"

"Because I'm not Alfred Lunt," I said. "It's not as easy as it seems."

"Well," said Tim, "I'm not you, but if I ever get to play Petruchio I'm going to swipe *all* your stuff."

"Flattery," I said, "will get you *some*where."

Cordelia spoke. "Oh, and how about that Curtis and Grumio scene?" She went into her man's voice and said, as Curtis,

"Is she so hot, the shrew, as she is reported?"

CORDELIA?

TIM *(as Grumio)*
She was, good Curtis, before this frost. But thou knowest winter tames man, woman, and beast for it hath tamed my old master and my new mistress and myself, fellow Curtis.

CORDY
Away, you three-inch fool! I am no beast.

TIM
Am I but three inches? Why, thy thorn is a foot, and so long am I at the least.

Pam managed, "All right, that's enough."

They had me worried. "I'll talk to Peter," I said. "Maybe we'll cut that."

"Down to *two* inches?" asked Cordy.

"That's enough, I said!" yelled Pam, but she could not refrain from joining in the general laughter.

We were having a good time. Another Jack Daniel's. Two more ales.

The evening ended merrily. The following morning, however, was to be less thrilling.

When we got home after the diner, Pam asked, "Do you think what I think?"

"I think so."

"Romance or *summer* romance?"

"Who can tell? They just seemed like two people having a good time with each other."

"But what about that cheeseburger, doesn't that

tell you something?"

"More than I want to know."

"And you don't think Tim would be so foolish as to . . . I mean, would he want to jeopardize his relationship with *us?*"

"Hard to say. Depends on the temperature. If they're solidly stuck on each other they're not going to give a damn about us. Or what we think. Or say."

"Oh, it must be just a fling," said Pam. "What with her going off to Texas in the fall. They both know that."

"I think I'm getting a migraine," I said.

"Have another Jack Daniel's," said Pam. "You've only had five."

Both Tim and Cordelia came late to rehearsal that following morning. She, about twenty minutes; he, a little over half an hour. They both apologized profusely to the director and to the company. Cordelia explained that she had slipped in the shower and twisted her ankle. She remembered to limp slightly for the rest of the day. It was the best acting I had ever seen her do. Tim stuck to the old reliable alarm-clock-didn't-go-off syndrome.

I had the assistant stage manager bring a couple of chicken salad sandwiches into Pam's dressing room when we broke for lunch and we held a whispered— or at least softly spoken—conversation.

"What do you think now?" I asked.

"You first. I'm in a state."

"Me, too. So you."

"All right."

"I think your Mr. Wakeman is a—"

"*My* Mr. Wakeman? What do you mean by that?"

"You brought him up here."

"*We,* baby. *We.*"

"Oh, what's the difference? I think he's knocked her over."

"And let's hope not 'up.'"

"So you agree."

"To a point."

"How do we know *she* didn't knock *him* over? Why is it always the boy's fault?"

"Boy? Some boy; the son of a bitch is over thirty."

"All right—man. Why is it always the man's fault?"

"Jesus," said Pam, "we sound like we're on the David Susskind show. Let's cut it out, y'mind?"

"Not at all."

"We've got to *do* something."

"Right," I said. "Or nothing."

"Right," she said. "Now if it's something, *you* do it. And if it's nothing, *I'll* do it."

"Well, *that* seems fair enough."

"Does your sandwich taste like cough syrup?" she asked. "Mine does."

"No. Mine's *good*. Tastes more like blood."

"Let's throw them away and get an Almond Joy, what do you say?"

"Two," I said. "I want one of my own, like the grownups."

We disposed of the sandwiches which were truly foul and walked out to the coffee shop in search of candy bars—both aware that we were carefully avoiding further discussion of the problem.

Candy bars in hand, we went for a walk.

"All right," said Pam finally. "A fact to face. Cordelia Standish, aged eighteen, is sleeping with Timothy Wakeman, thirty-something."

"Now, we don't actually *know* that, do we?"

"I think we do."

"All right. Suppose. So now what?"

"The question is: Is it any of our business?"

"I suppose not. Not in nineteen eighty anyway."

"And there's no way to change *that,* is there?"

"Do you mind the whole company knowing?"

"I wonder. They do, of course. Did you dig the snickering contest they had going there this morning? After the two of them showed up late?"

"That cheeseburger last night should've told us."

"It did."

"Some, not all."

I stopped walking, so did Pam.

"Idea," I said, "at last."

"Yes."

"We shut up, say nothing, go on as before— precisely—with both of them."

"That's the idea?" asked Pam incredulously.

"No. Hold it."

"I'm holding."

"We simply wait for her—or him, or both of them—to bring it up with *us.*"

"What if they don't?"

"They will. You'll see. I bet she takes it up with you, and he with me."

"Damn," said Pam.

I was wrong. I would have lost my bet. Rehearsals continued. We made it a point to have as many meals and meetings as possible with Cordy and Tim. At times I worried that we were rather overdoing the heartiness of it all. Before long our troublesome twosome began leaving the theater together and arriving together with regularity.

Then, three nights before the opening of *Earnest*, the subject came up as though by design. But I had erred in my prediction. Cordy took it up with me right after rehearsal one late afternoon, while Tim went to see Pam.

"Daddy, I suppose you know about me and Tim."

"I see you give yourself top billing. Good instinct."

"*Do* you? Know, I mean."

"Know what?"

"You know," she said softly and meaningfully, "that Tim and I are lovers."

"I do *now*."

"Do you mind?"

"Not if you're happy, love."

"I am."

"You don't think he's a little old for you?"

"No. I think *I'm* a little young for *him*. But he

doesn't mind."

"It just takes a little getting used to, darling, that's all. You can understand that."

"Of course, Daddy. Tim's telling Mother. In fact, this whole *telling* thing is *his* idea."

"He's a gentleman."

"Yes, I've never met one before."

"Me?"

"Well, I never really met *you,* did I?"

"Good shot," I said, and we smiled together.

She came to me then, sat on my lap and embraced me.

"Wow!" she said. "I haven't done this for a long time. It's nice."

"Yes, it is."

"And I don't know . . . but I think I should tell you . . . no . . . I mean, I think I want . . . no . . . I want to tell you that . . ." She stopped.

"That what?" I prompted.

She buried her head in my shoulder and said, "That there never was anyone before Tim. I mean not really. A little movie theater smooching, a lot of boring sofa-wrestling—that's all."

"Any prognosis?" I asked.

She laughed. "You make it sound like a disease."

"It is, in a way. Love."

She left my lap, moved away and turned back to me.

"Did I say I was in love?"

"Didn't you? Aren't you?"

CORDELIA?

"How would I know?"

"You said 'lovers.'"

"But that doesn't mean love, does it?"

"You tell *me."*

"It doesn't. It means we've begun a sexual relationship, and it's beautiful and exciting and we enjoy each other—but Romeo and Juliet—no—if that's what you mean."

"All right."

"I'm not saying it might not happen some day, maybe even with Tim, but—oh, hell, now you've got me all mixed up."

"Cordy, you're the least mixed up little lady I've ever known in all my life."

She moved closer to me and touched my head. "If I ask you an indiscreet question, will you give me an indiscreet answer?"

"Yes. Your mother and I were lovers before we were married, yes."

She laughed and spun about. "But that wasn't going to be my question, wise guy, so I got that one free, huh?"

"What *was* the question?"

"Did Lynn and Miss Laurette tell you when they—"

"How many times have I asked you not to call her Miss Laurette?"

"Four hundred and sixteen."

"Then why do you persist?"

"Because I'm a bitch, I suppose."

61

"Will you stop it?"

"I'll try."

"No, don't try—*do.*"

"All right. Well, did they?"

"No, they did not."

"But did you know anyway?"

"I did with Lynn—"

"How?"

"When she decided to go off to Aspen and ski with Tommy instead of coming home for Christmas."

"And how old was *she?*"

"Now, let's see, that was Christmas, seventy-seven, so she would've been nineteen."

"A late bloomer, huh? And Miss—sorry—and Laurette?"

"No idea. She may still be—well, so far as I know."

"Would you like to?"

"What?"

"Know. I could tell you a thing or two. Or three."

"Don't."

"It's what I hate about her—well, *one* of the things I hate about her—that airy, arty, actressy pose. Above it all, and the truth is—"

"Hold it."

"You don't want to hear the truth?"

"Not from you, no."

"Why not?"

"Because you're biased."

CORDELIA?

"The truth is, she's promiscuous. She had four men before her sixteenth birthday, and one *on* her sixteenth birthday."

"Cordy!"

"It's true!"

"I hope you can *prove* all this! God, how I hate gossip."

"She *told* me. And Lynn, too. Boasting."

"Fantasizing, more likely. Teasing you."

"She showed us letters, even."

"I'd very much like to terminate this conversation."

"And by the way, you're wrong about Lynn, too."

"Oh, my God!"

"It happened *long* before Aspen and Tommy."

I regarded her. She seemed, all at once, a stranger. She didn't look like Pam at all. Where did I ever get *that* misguided notion? She *copied* Pam—in voice, in gesture, expression and manner; in dress, in hairdress and makeup (when Pam changed lipstick, so did she). She imitated Pam's musical laugh and sudden smile—sneezed and coughed and belched like Pam. That was it, I suppose, but standing here now she was someone else entirely. Herself? And who was she?

My next line came out before I meant it to. "You really *are* a bitch, aren't you?"

"Aren't we all?" she asked loftily. "But I have a sweet side, too."

"I wish you'd use it more."

"I will, Daddy, that's a promise. You're a great guy."

She kissed my cheek and was gone.

Before the first dress rehearsal that night Pam and I had dinner alone.

"I've got a lot to tell you," I said.

"Ditto."

"Shall we do it now or wait?"

"Are you out of your gourd? We've got a dress in an hour and a half—*less*. I'm not all that secure with the words as it is. All I need is a crisis to distract me and I'll go right back into my Edith Evans imitation that you despise so."

"Anything but that! *Anything!*"

She rehearsed to herself, mumbling Lady Bracknell's long speech as she spooned her soup, no mean feat. After a time, she looked up.

"Do you think it's a mistake to have children? For actors and actresses I mean?"

"It may be a mistake for anyone," I said, "the way I feel today."

"Bad session, huh?"

"How was yours?"

"Worse."

The first night of *The Importance of Being Earnest* went extremely well—no thanks to me. I simply could not get going and felt off-balance all evening. Timing, ragged; reflexes sluggish. But such is the strength of that comic masterpiece that the audience was unaware of my lapses. Another worry was Cordelia. She looked a dream, of course, and spoke up nicely, but there was only an actress there, not a human being. Was I being too hard on her? Possibly. Expecting too much? Yes. She was, after all, a tyro, and would have all summer to play it in.

Seven

The day after *Earnest* opened, Pam and I finally got a chance to exchange reports.

"I told our lover-in-law plainly," she said, "that I thought him too old for Cordy."

"I did, too. Told *her,* I mean."

"He said he agreed with me, but that there was nothing he could do about it. He promised to take care of her and try to make her happy and hoped we'd understand that there was nothing casual about the whole thing—that it was serious."

"Did you mention marriage?"

"No, but he did."

"And?"

"—said he had high hopes for the future, but that he meant to leave the decision to her."

"Not us?"

"No. And what did our little femme fatale have to offer?"

"Lip, mostly. She didn't ask, she just told. Swear to God, Pam, I've never felt so elderly. She seemed thirty-three years old."

"Maybe she is."

"What do you think is going to happen?"

"God knows."

"No, He doesn't. No one does, not even them."

"I do. They'll have a swinging summer, and come fall, she'll be off with the animals. They'll phone each other and write, he'll fly out, she'll fly in—and in time it'll fold its tents like the Arabs and silently steal away."

"And *as* silently steal away," I corrected.

"Thank you."

"Except that it won't."

"Wait and see."

We waited. And saw.

The following week *The Taming of the Shrew* opened and my professional judgment about Cordelia was reinforced. Again she played cleanly and charmingly but without—what's the word?—without the spark. Again I resolved to give her more time.

When the season was a little over two weeks old, Tim moved in with Cordelia. We had rented a comfortable apartment for her within walking distance of the theater. When she came over one day

CORDELIA?

and borrowed Pam's copy of *The New York Times Cookbook,* we understood. All of us—Pam, I, Lynn and Laurette—are interested in food and cooking, but we could never get Cordelia to join in.

"Cooking," she once said, "is a dead key on my piano."

Her life was changing rapidly, but not at the theater.

There she still got neither better nor worse but continued to give the kind of preserved-in-amber performances that madden me.

After the second Saturday night, with both plays on and the prospect at last of a glorious gaping Sunday ahead, Pam and I went off to a favorite haunt, The Windsor Arms in Toronto. We had reserved our favorite suite and our usual table in the Brasserie, and after a drive through the moonlight, settled in for a whole night and a whole day and another night then half another day of lolling and loafing, eating and drinking and lovemaking. And a few long walks. In the course of one of them I voiced my disquietude about Cordelia's acting. Pam reluctantly agreed.

"I've been waiting patiently," she said, "or maybe *impatiently* for it to happen—to begin to happen. It hasn't. And I'm beginning to think it's not going to."

"Could it be this goddamned affair she's all wrapped up in? Her first, remember. Love affairs can be pretty distracting."

"All of *mine* were," said Pam.

"What a memory!"

"I suppose," she said, "if we tried to help her—either one of us—it would only make matters worse."

"I'm afraid so. It *must* be the affair. Otherwise, what could it be?"

Pam took a deep breath and said, "How about no talent?"

I was stunned. "That thought has never occurred to me."

"It has to me," said Pam, "and remember we forced her into this job."

"She's not really interested in it—let alone passionate. Hey! Maybe that's the trouble. Like mechanical screwing."

"You put things so daintily, dear."

"She's still going to be a vet, God help us."

"You think so?"

"Of course."

"You don't think this Tim thing is going to make a difference in the end?"

"Oh, come on, you know better than that. You've seen dozens of these summer romances. Especially theater summer romances. What was that catch line? 'They loved each other madly but the show closed.'"

"I'm not so sure, they seem pretty involved. And happy, I must admit."

"So was I when I was eighteen."

"Aren't you now?"

"Not in the same way, no."

"Why not?"

"Wrinkles," she said.

"I love your wrinkles."
"You should, you gave them to me."
"Let's go to bed," I suggested, "and be together. You always look about fifteen afterward."
"You better watch out, mister. You'll get arrested."

She did look fifteen afterward. Fourteen.

Dom Perignon with dinner. It always sets me afloat. New ideas come up out of the bubbles, mystically.

"You know what I worry about sometimes in the dark?" I asked.

"What?"

"What if she gets pregnant?"

"Don't be silly. Girls don't get pregnant anymore. Where've you been? Not unless they want to, or get drunk."

"Well—"

"Not Cordy."

We began to discuss the superlative food and thank fortune, got off the subject for the rest of the evening.

Eight

Driving back to Stratford the following day, a new concept that had struck me in the night came to fruition and I decided to try it out on Pam.

"I was thinking in the night, love—"

"You were also snoring."

"All that food."

"*What* were you thinking?"

"Could she be doing what she's doing purposely?"

"Doing what?"

"Holding back, not giving out, not playing as well as she could if she wanted to."

"Why would she do that?"

"To get us off her back, don't you see? To get us to accept the fact that she's going to Texas to pursue her own plan."

Pam laughed. "That's quite a flight, my boy. She'd

have to be damn good to bring *that* off."

"It's possible, though. David Merrick once told me about Bob Redford's first job on Broadway. It was a comedy called, I think, *Sunday in New York,* or something like that, and Redford mortgaged his house in L.A. to get the dough for the trip east, just to read. So David says he came in and read for the lead and knocked everybody out and the director and the author were ready to sign him, but David says he was still hoping to get a big name for the part, so they asked Redford to read for another part, the second lead, and he did, and the effect was so negative that they all thought they'd reacted wrongly to the first reading. So they asked him to read the lead again and he did, and he was great again. Well, eventually he got the part and made a big hit and was off to a career. And David says that years later he ran into Redford in the Polo Lounge. They had a drink and talked and David recalled that audition and said, 'I never understood how you could've been so good and so bad in the same hour.' 'Because,' said Redford, 'I wanted the *lead,* not the *second* lead.'"

"Interesting," said Pam, "but with all due respect to our own dear Queen, she's no Robert Redford."

Still, the notion haunted me. I watched Cordy carefully for the next few nights and learned exactly nothing.

The bombshell fell and exploded between the Saturday matinee and night performances exactly two weeks before the end of the season. Cordy came into Pam's room. I was there.

As a rule, I am anti-trousers, slacks or jeans on girls. I respond to femininity, and to legs. But Cordy wore her jeans differently somehow. Sexually.

She asked, "You guys doing your Toronto thing tonight?"

"Yes," I said, "why?"

"Could I come with you?"

I saw Pam's face in her dressing-table mirror. It tightened with sudden apprehension; but, consummate actress that she is, she spoke calmly and clearly. "Why, of course, love. What a splendid surprise!"

"Fine," I managed to get out.

"See you," said Cordy and started out. She stopped and asked, "Here or house?"

"Whichever you like," said Pam. "We have to stop there for a few minutes."

"House, then." She was gone.

"Oh, *dear! Oh,* dear!" said Pam. "It's over."

"Now don't take on. It was inevitable."

"But there're two weeks to go—what could have happened?"

"A thousand things."

"Maybe just a temporary spat?"

"How the hell would I know, Pam?" I yelled. "Sorry."

Matters became even more confused as we drove

to Toronto. We had no sooner hit the freeway when Cordelia began to sing. She obliged with the entire score of *A Little Night Music*. She is not much of a singer, but her memory is prodigious.

"Any requests?" she asked when she had finished the finale.

"Yes," I said, "a little night silence."

Pam said, "Remember that great money-making idea I once had?"

"Which one?" asked Cordy.

"The one where I wanted there to be a slot on every jukebox in America—that when you put in a quarter, you got five minutes of absolute quiet."

"Oh, *that* one," said Cordelia. "Whatever happened to it?"

"Someone stole it," said Pam.

"You had another one I liked even better."

"Oh?"

"That one about every theater having two box offices, one in the back where you pay to get in and another one in the front where you can pay to get out."

"Forgot that one," said Pam.

We drove on for a time. I knew that Pam was as anxious as I was to hear the news—whatever it was—but we knew better than to ask.

Cordelia began to sing again, Stevie Wonder this time, and we joined in as we had done a few summers earlier.

The trip went from song to silence and back—but little or no speech. Nor was it forthcoming during supper, although many subjects were covered.

We took her up to her room on the same floor as ours, and saw that she was comfortable. We all kissed good-night, and just as we were leaving, she said, "I need a couple of hours with you tomorrow, anytime—morning, not too early, afternoon, evening—I don't want to be in the way."

"How could you ever be in the way, you goose," I asked. "What do you say to after lunch?"

"Perfect," she said.

Back in our suite, Pam said, "The goddam suspense is killing me."

"Why do I keep thinking pregnant?" I asked.

"Because you're a neurotic half-wit, is why. If it were that, she'd be seeing a doctor, not us."

"Marriage?"

"Not a chance. She's too intelligent to do it at eighteen. Listen, she may not be much of an actress, but she's smarter than the other two put together. I'm the one who's had the long talks with her. She's amazing."

We all met for a long leisurely midday meal, and afterward went back up to the suite.

We sat, she stood.

"Well," she said finally. "Here goes. Texas is out."

We were too stunned to speak.

"I'm really sorry about one thing, Dad."

"What's that?" I asked.

"The seven-hundred-and-fifty-buck fee you put

up. It isn't returnable. I raised hell with the registrar on the phone, but it was no go."

"Forget it," I said.

"What *are* you going to do?" asked Pam.

"I'm going to New York. Tim's got a neat apartment on Barrow Street and I'm going to move in with him and get going."

"You still haven't said—get going where? What?"

She struck a ridiculous overdramatic pose and exclaimed, "I'm going on the stage! My people are against it—social you know—but I want to act! I don't want to be an actress, as some put it—no—I want to *act!*"

Talk about act. For the next ten minutes Pam and I extended ourselves beyond our capabilities. We outdid ourselves as well as one another reacting enthusiastically and happily to this announcement which, in view of what we had learned during the summer, was a near tragedy.

When the first excitement had subsided, I took charge, putting forth a last straw I had grasped during the noise.

"Listen to me, Cordy, there are one or two subjects I know something about, and this is one of them. Acting. The theater. Tim, fine. Barrow Street. O.K. But listen. Go to Juilliard and train."

"If you can get in," said Pam.

"No," said Cordy.

"Cordy," I said, "you're terrific, you proved that up here the way I knew you would, but it's a tough world out there, the competition is overwhelming.

CORDELIA?

Get some more training while you can, while you're young enough."

"I've been all through this with Tim—he doesn't agree with you at all. He said four years at drama school is a waste—especially for me, with my connections."

"Jesus," I shouted, "who do you think knows more about it, me or Tim?"

"Tim."

"What?!"

"You're way up there in the horse latitudes, Dad. Tim is on the ground where things are different. He says I can take classes—the way he does—but mainly the thing to do is to get work."

"What kind of work?" asked Pam.

"Whatever. Commercials, stock, TV, off-Broadway, off-off, showcase, regional. Go for it, you know. And pray."

I held up both hands. "Wait a second, I suggest a five-minute recess."

I went to the bathroom. When I returned Pam was looking out the window, Cordelia was stretched out on the sofa. We resumed.

"First of all," I said, "connections. Well and good. Of course, we can *get* you interviews and auditions, maybe even jobs. We can get them for you, but only *you* can *keep* them and that means being prepared, trained. Look at Laurette—"

"*You* look at her."

"Now, Cordy—"

"Come on," she said, "let's not beat around the

bush. I know you think I'm not much good—as an actress, I mean. But I don't do—and I'm not going to do—the kind of acting *you* do. It's a different style, another approach. Modern. I'm going to make it just fine. Don't you worry."

"Where did you ever get the idea," I asked, "that we think you're no good—as an actress?"

"It's in the air. In these matters, it isn't always what you say, it's what you *fail* to say—and you two have failed to say quite a lot."

"Cordy—" Pam began.

"Never mind. It's all right. You're entitled to your opinion even if it's wrong."

"Listen, daughter dear," I said, "thanks for the best news so far this year. I'm thrilled."

"So am I," said Pam.

Cordelia, in a flat, businesslike way said, "Now I'm going to call Tim and tell him I've told you, then I'm going to the zoo and then I'd like to take you two out to dinner. Japanese O.K.? I hear there's a good one."

"Fine," I said.

"What time?"

"Drinks, seven, downstairs?"

"Splendid," she said.

She embraced Pam, gave me a tired, eighteen-year-old kiss and left.

Pam and I looked at each other for the longest time.

She spoke first. "My grandmother used to say, 'Little children, little troubles; big children, big troubles.'"

"Your grandmother," I said, "was probably Socrates. Fasten your seat belts."

"Love conquers all," she said. "I just made that up."

"Not bad," I said. "Not bad at all. By the way, in matters of predictions and judgments I've been batting zilch of late. How can I be so wrong about everything?"

"But don't you find that interesting?" asked Pam.

"What?"

"Being surprised at yourself all the time."

"No, it's jarring."

Nine

The season ended. There was a sumptuous celebration. Singing and dancing and tears and a great deal of drinking. It may have been the last that caused me to suggest to Peter that we come back the following season to do *Private Lives* and *King Lear*.

"Smashing!" he said. *"Lear* and . . . what else did you say?"

"I forget."

"It was something, though. *Lear* and something. Was it King something?"

"No, you fathead! It's *King Lear*."

For some reason, this sent him into gales of laughter.

"What the hell's so funny?" I asked. "That we can't even remember the name of the second play? Between us can't?"

"No," he said. "I just remembered a great crack somebody made about somebody. About one of our superstars—great, but gay—when it was announced that he was coming to America to play King Richard II and somebody said, 'I'm goddam sick and tired of seeing English queens play English kings!'"

"Private Lives," I said.

"What about them?"

"That's the Noel second Coward play."

"You didn't laugh at English queens, English kings."

"What?"

"The joke."

"I didn't hear it. I was trying to think of the second play."

"Private Lives," he said, "by Coward Noel."

"What's it about?" I asked.

He replied seriously. *"Private Lives.* One of the all-time greats. Divorced couple. He remarries. She remarries. Two honeymoons. Same hotel in the South of France. Adjoining balconies. They meet, fall in love again—or still. Run away together. And it goes on from there."

"Why, that's the most outrageous thing I ever heard!"

"What?"

"It's a direct steal from *Private Lives* by Noel Coward!"

It was that sort of evening. A few drinks later, we sat in the back of someone's limousine and continued to plan.

CORDELIA?

Peter leaned forward and said excitedly, "I've got the goddamndest most spectacular idea in the entire history of show business. Or the theater. Or Shakespeare. Check one. Want to hear it?"

"If it's not too long."

"You're King Lear, right?"

"I certainly am. Would you care to see my I.D.?"

"And what has Lear got?"

"A beard."

"What else?"

"A jester. The Fool."

"What else? Come on—you know. Three . . . three . . ."

"Sisters!" I shouted.

"No, no, no! That's Chekhov. *He's* got three sisters. Not Chekhov. Lear. Lear's got three *daughters*."

"I know," I said. "Cordelia and Gonorrhea and Syphilis."

"No, *no, no!*" he yelled. "You're thinking of Sisyphus. *The Myth of Sisyphus*. That's another play altogether. Anyway, I don't want to do that one, it's too Greek."

"It's too Greek to me, too."

He studied me carefully for a time, then said, "Listen, Alan. Are you a little pissed?"

"Not a *little*, no."

"All right then, listen carefully. Turn on your hearing aid. Lear's got three daughters, right?"

"Right."

"And what have *you* got?"

"I don't know, what *have* I got? Oh, my God! Not *Sisyphus?* Where's my penicillin? These days it's no worse than a bad cold."

"Three daughters. That's what you've got."

"I have?"

"Of course. Laurette, Lynn, Cordelia. One, two, three. And all actresses. Professional actresses."

"Well, I'll be damned."

"So are you with me so far? Now get this inspired concept! You play Lear and your three daughters play your three daughters. Are you holding on to something?"

"You mean Lear's three daughters!"

"Yes. Talk about fortuitous!"

"Listen," I asked. "Are you a little pissed?"

"Not a little, no. There has never been an idea as brilliant as this. Not since the Oliviers did the two Cleopatras in rep. Shakesberg and Shaw. And, what's more, all your daughters *look* like you."

"I know. The lucky devils."

"Well, what do you think of it? Of the idea? The concept?"

"It's good," I said. "But it's no good."

"Why not?"

"Because if the girls play the girls, you nut, what does Pam play?"

"I was coming to that, you nut. *Another* revolutionary idea. Pam plays the great part of the Fool. And steals the show, probably."

"Thanks awfully," I said, sounding like Gielgud.

We went on babbling in this surrealist vein until

we fell asleep. The owner of the car woke us up and was surprisingly decent about the whole matter.

Most drunken ideas seem embarrassing in the morning, but Peter was even more firm when we continued to discuss it the following day.

He had even gotten to Pam and sold her his scheme.

The three of us met for lunch and further chat. We all had casting ideas. Tim as Edmund. What period? Conventional, or try an angle? Designer? We went on into the late afternoon.

At length, Peter, flushed with anticipatory creation, said, "Well then, the die is cast."

"Yes," said Pam. "Now if the cast doesn't die, we're all set."

Ten

In New York, at a meeting with Tim and Cordy, we told them that I was going to do *Lear* again.

"Is that a good idea, Daddy?" asked Cordy. "Didn't you bomb out in it once?"

"Yes," I said, "but not twice."

I then offered the part of Edmund to Tim who jumped at it.

Both he and Cordy thought the idea of Pam as the Fool was super. I took a deep breath and said to my daughter, "And what would you think of Cordelia as Cordelia?"

Instead of replying, she burst into tears.

We went to "21" to celebrate.

Cordelia took my hand and asked, "Daddy, will

you help me? I can be good. I know it. If only someone will help me. I know I've been a pain, but I'm going to change—"

"Not too much, please," said Tim.

"I'll coach," she said. "Get me a coach."

"Not so fast. All that's up to Peter. He's the director, remember."

"I'm going to work my *ass* off!" said Cordy.

"Please don't," said Pam. "You're going to need it for the part."

"And can I have the French maid in *Private Lives?*"

"Only if Tim agrees to play Victor," I said.

I shall not attempt to describe the next ten minutes, but they were euphoric for all.

Eleven

Peter wrote to me from London:

Partner dear,

Your Cordy (she of the expensive habits) got me on the overseas blower yesterday to get permission for coaching. I could not be more delighted. As you know, I love directing plays, and hate directing players. *However*. I would not wish her to fall into the hands of some traditionalist who might lead her into temptation. What she needs is work on voice and speech and articulation. Also a sense of the rhythm and the poetry. Perhaps she should work *off* of the part, study and read Juliet for example.

Edith Evans long advocated reading French aloud when playing Shakespeare. She claimed that it was an incomparable exercise for the lips and tongue and jaws and all the organs of speech. Edith was an inspired eccentric and all of her notions deserve attention. Did I ever tell you that when I offered her Lady Macbeth opposite Richardson, she turned it down? Why? "Because," she said, "I could never reconcile Lady Macbeth's behavior with the Scottish sense of hospitality." (!) Thus, the greatest British actress of her time, and a perfect Lady Macbeth, never did play it. Oh, you actors! But another time, she said something profound. I had criticized her wide, active participation in extra-theatre activity and travel and causes and committees. "But, ducky," she said, "I have always believed that Art should be what is left over from Life!"

Not bad, what?

About Cordy and coaching: Would you, could you consider taking it on personally? You would surely be the best for her. Pam would too, of course, but it's long been my experience that men should be coached by women and vice versa in order to avoid picking up quirks, mannerisms, et al.

The West End is booming just now along with

all the Nationals, so continue to pray.

Perhaps a quick Concorde over in late November? Might we have a weekend? Where will you be?

>Love to you and all your women,
>Peter

I showed Cordy the letter and we agreed to set up a schedule as soon as my own plans were firm. Pam and I were going to do a play for Richmond Crinkley at Lincoln Center that would take ten weeks—four rehearsal, and six playing. We then hoped to book a tour of *Private Lives,* so that when the summer came, we could put our full attention on *Lear.*

Plans, as they all too infrequently do, began to fall into place neatly. Laurette was delighted to learn that she would have a job soon after finishing at Juilliard. Lynn, for a time, was a stumbling block.

"I'm a dancer, not an actress," she insisted.

"But Lynnie," said Pam, "it's not permanent. You're not being asked to abandon your career. And anyway, being an actress—a real actress—won't that make you a better dancer?" (She generally put things to the children in the form of questions rather than personal opinions or judgments. Brilliant.)

"I can't stop dancing for a whole summer, Mother, you know better than that."

"But you're not being asked to, love. You can take class every day up there—"

"No," said Lynn, and left the room.

We began looking for a replacement. Peter returned from London and insisted upon achieving a physical resemblance between the daughter and me.

I pointed out that Cordelia resembled her mother more than she did me.

"No, no," said Peter. "There's enough of you there to work on. Have you ever heard of makeup? Also that's all the more reason why I want to get a dead ringer to replace Lynn. Damn! You're certain we can't get her to change her mind?"

"You can try, Peter, but it's a lost cause."

"Blast," he said. "Blast!"

"And, Peter, let's not get carried away. Let's get a good actress instead of trying for a clone. We'll wind up with a klutz who looks like me. So what?"

"Look, ol' cock, there are eight thousand unemployed actresses in New York City, and if I ask Howie or Barry to send up six girls, all five-three, and all with blue eyes and button noses and freckles, they'd have sixteen up overnight. We'll find her. Relax. Anyway, we have plenty of time."

As it happened, Peter was overconfident. The plenty of time went by and no suitable candidates appeared. The ones who bore a resemblance—ever so slight or surprisingly great—were not much good.

And the ones who auditioned brilliantly could not possibly be daughters of mine. Too tall, too short, too different, too everything.

Lincoln Center rehearsals began. Simultaneously, we were putting together the *Private Lives* tour, in addition to which Cordy would not let me off the coaching hook and insisted on finding hours in my insane schedule to work with her.

It was quite an autumn.

The coaching sessions were less than completely successful and I began to think that perhaps it was my fault rather than hers.

Her approach was entirely too intellectual, pre-planned. I could not make her understand the necessity of letting go, of trusting her instincts.

"It's all too careful, darling. If you're going to be an actress, you can't be worried about making a mistake. You've got to take chances. Everybody who acts in public runs the risk of making a horse's ass out of himself or herself, but you've got to reach and be daring. Try things. If they're no good, you can always edit them out later, but give the director something to work with. Don't make him pull it out of you. Give him a flowing cornucopia of stuff and let him choose what he wants and delete what he doesn't want. Trust your instincts."

"I don't have any instincts," she said, "I have to know what I'm doing. And why."

"But that's what gets you to watching yourself, darling. And listening to yourself. You can't be actress and audience at the same time. Anyone who doesn't understand schizophrenia, doesn't understand acting. There are always two. The actor and the character. The actor working the character in the way that those geniuses work the Muppets. You never see them, aren't even *aware* of them, but they're *there*. And the strange thing is that sometimes the puppets begin to work the puppeteers. Just as the character begins to use the actor."

"I don't get it, Daddy. I just don't *get* it."

"You will," I said, but did not believe it for a minute.

We began rehearsals for Lincoln Center in late October, opened on November 23rd, and played through the first of the year.

Because of a series of complicated booking problems which I did not comprehend—and do not to this day—it was necessary for us to go into rehearsal with *Private Lives* during the last two weeks of Lincoln Center. It was a hell time, aggravated by the fact that Pam blamed me entirely for the whole mess.

"You and your harebrained schemes!" she shouted at me one evening in the taxi on the way to the theater from a six-hour rehearsal. "What I *ought* to be doing right now is going home to lie in a warm bath for half an hour and then have a nap before a beautiful dinner. Instead, you've got me gulping a tongue-and-Swiss while I make up to go on and give a tired, forced performance and collapse. You're the bloody overdoer of all time, you know that, don't you? You're not happy unless you're doing two things at once—three! I'm surprised you don't try to read a script while we're balling. And speaking of that, do you know how long it's been since—? *I* do. You could've avoided this jam if you'd stood up to them and not caved in when they bluffed you about canceling. Right?"

I said nothing because she was right.

I had other things on my mind as well. Cordelia.

Even in the small part of Louise, the little French maid in *Private Lives,* she was less than satisfactory. The externals were fine. She had gotten herself up to look actually French. She went to French movies endlessly and found gestures and facial expressions that worked well. She learned her whole part in French and asked Peter if she could rehearse it in French from time to time. He agreed. It was interesting and enjoyable. But the work was consistently manufactured and bloodless.

I asked Peter, a true theater animal, what he thought.

"You don't want the truth, do you?" he asked.

"In this case, yes."

"I don't think she's interested in acting. She's interested in l-u-v."

"Can't she be in both?"

"Certainly, but she isn't."

"How can you tell, Peter? I'd like to know. Just for my own education."

"Attitude. The questions she asks. The questions she *doesn't* ask. She never even watches rehearsals except when Tim's on."

"Jesus!" I said, "what are we going to do about *Lear?*"

"Worry," he said. "How's the coaching coming?"

"Grim," I said.

"Well, sufficient unto the day. Let's get this one on and then we'll go to work. Nothing's impossible."

"Don't you believe it," I said. "What I'm doing right now is impossible."

We opened *Private Lives* in Wilmington, then went on to the Eisenhower in Washington for a five-week run. All went well—reviews, business, performances. Little or no progress in Cordy's work, however.

Moreover, now that I had more time for coaching, she seemed less interested and more unavailable.

"Would you like Tim to take over?" I asked her one afternoon. "I can assure you my feelings won't be hurt. Whatever's best for you. Maybe Tim?"

"Oh, no!"

"Why not?"

"Because I already asked him and he turned me down."

"Did he say why?"

"Yes, he said he thought it would put a strain on our relationship."

"Bright fellow."

"But why did you ask? Are you getting sick of it?"

CORDELIA?

"No, but I get the feeling you are."

"Well, it *is* pretty boring, isn't it?"

"No. It *shouldn't* be. But look, what would you think of this? Why don't you learn the part of Juliet?"

"The whole thing?" She was horrified.

"Sure, why not? And we'll work on scenes. Remember, that was one of the methods Peter suggested."

"All right."

"So no more sessions until you're ready."

"With Juliet, you mean?"

"Yes."

"Good!"

Pam and I saw little of Cordelia and Tim except at the theater. They were enjoying the wonders of Washington—the Freer, the Smithsonian, the National, the Library of Congress, the White House and, needless to say, the zoo.

From Washington we went to Chicago for a six-week engagement at the Blackstone. Everything good again.

We all stayed at the Whitehall, and on the second day, trouble.

"Dad, I've got this idea you're going to hate, but hear me out. O.K.?"

"O.K."

"Instead of Tim in his room and me in mine,

couldn't we have a suite like you and Mom? It wouldn't cost a penny more. In fact, a little cheaper, and so much more comfortable, and it *is* for six weeks. Don't you think it makes sense? I mean to be perfectly practical."

"Is that the pitch?"

"Yes."

"The whole pitch? You're finished?"

"I think so."

"The answer, I'm sorry to say, is no. What's more, I wish you hadn't asked."

"Reasons?" she asked. "Or reason."

"Obvious."

"This is nineteen eighty-one, you know."

"So I'm told."

"So?"

"So, no."

"We did in Stratford."

"Entirely different."

"I don't see how."

"A tiny community. A company atmosphere. This is a big city, a public hotel. Newspapers. Your age. Discretion. I'm sorry. I know it sounds unconvincing, but it goes against the grain."

"Whose grain?"

"Mine."

"And what about *mine?*"

I could see I was facing a battle. She stood up and I felt the space between us become charged with the tension of the coming tantrum.

"But don't you see how *stupid* this whole thing is?" she said tightly. "How goddam *wasteful?* I'm never *in* that room of mine, so what's the sense of paying for it? Just as a blind? Is a blind worth a hundred and ten bucks a day, for God's sake? All right, all *right!* I know what we'll do. We'll move. We'll go to the Blackstone and get a suite—nearer the theater anyhow."

"I wouldn't like that, Cordelia."

"No? Well, I *would!*"

"Now simmer down. This is one time you're not going to have your way."

"Any bets?" she yelled defiantly.

"No screaming."

"That wasn't screaming," she said quietly. "This is."

Whereupon she emitted a startling, horrendous, blood-curdling scream that brought Pam rushing in from the bedroom, stark naked.

"What in the name of—?" she asked.

"God *damn* it!" Cordy shouted. "I'm fed up with being treated like a child."

"Only when you behave like one," I said.

"What the hell's it all about?" asked Pam.

"Tell her," I said.

"*You* tell her."

"Oh, no. You. It's *your* big idea."

I saw a sudden glimpse of devious hope in her eye. She stepped toward me and asked, "If *she* says O.K. will *you* give in?"

101

I don't know why I said yes, but I did.

"Fine."

She turned to Pam and proceeded to outline her plan, but this time she did it in a way that made it seem somehow even more logical and reasonable. What a skillful manipulator! As she reached the end, I was certain that Pam would acquiesce. Wrong again.

Pam simply said, "Don't be ridiculous," and went back into the bedroom.

Cordy began to charge out of the room, but I stopped her.

"Listen, missy, let me remind you that in spite of the fact that you think of yourself as a liberated, sophisticated lady, you're only eighteen years old."

"Almost nineteen," she said.

"Almost doesn't count. Right now—as you stand there blazing and hating me—you're still my daughter, which means that I'm responsible for you and your actions and I'm accepting that responsibility, and by the way, you might tell Tim that I'm damned disappointed in him."

"He doesn't even *know* about it. It was all my idea. I was going to tell him later when it was all set."

"I see."

"May I go now?"

"If you want to."

"I do."

"Very well, then."

"And I *don't* hate you. I never could."

CORDELIA?

She was gone.

Now I'm getting nervous. Worse, I'm unnerved. Terrified. I want very much to stop setting down this account. In fact, I doubt that I can go on. I can't.

Twelve

I begin again. It has been two months and two days since I abandoned this project. I have had many literally sleepless nights. I have had tense days when I felt brittle enough to break at a touch. I have seen Dr. Fred Plum, the great neurologist. I have gone on four different medications. Nothing has worked.

I went back to Cincinnati to see Ben again. He asked me how far I had gotten with the account. I said about halfway. He urged me to go on and finish it, and pointed out that I had no other course in view of the fact that everything else I had tried up to then was unsuccessful and that I was still of the opinion that it was not a subject I could discuss with anyone, not even with him.

We went out for a walk.

"I thought it was going well," I explained. "But then I got to the point where I simply couldn't face—well, certain things. And writing them out seemed to make them worse. You know what I mean? Fuzzy, unpleasant grey inside my head, but glaring awful shaming accusing black and white on the page."

"Don't give it up," he said. "You've come this far."

We walked two quiet blocks in the Sunday silence. All at once, to my surprise, I heard myself ask, "To what extent, Ben, do you think talent is hereditary?"

He laughed. "Now, now," he said. "You don't get me onto *that* one. Look at the trouble poor Lysenko got himself into."

"Who?"

"Lysenko—the Russian who claimed to have proved that characteristics developed by environment could be genetically transmitted. He died in disgrace."

"But *you* went into your father's profession, more or less, didn't you?"

"Yes."

"And by and large most children of actors and actresses go into the theater."

"Ah, yes," he said. "But are they all talented?"

"Not all, no."

"You see why it's a sticky subject? Almost impossible to pin down. Let me tell you a fascinating story." He stopped and laughed. "Whenever I said that to Woollcott, he'd snarl and say '*I'll* be the judge of that.' At any rate, here's the story: A couple in Bonn, Germany, many, many years ago had a child who proved to be mongoloid. The father was a depraved, diseased alcoholic, which may have accounted for it. The child, whom they named Ludwig, died after a few days. Their doctor advised them to have no more children, but they refused and produced a second child. They named this one Ludwig, too. Ludwig van Beethoven. They then proceeded to spawn six more children, all unexceptional and mostly cretins who died in infancy. Does that answer your question?"

We went back to his place and talked all afternoon, then went out and talked all through dinner. But I stopped when I began to suspect that he was beginning to fathom something about my problem.

Not too skillfully, I switched us over to *Hamlet* then and was spellbound for hours. I missed the last plane and had to spend the night in Cincinnati.

The next day, I picked up the thread of my account as best I could.

So here I am, back to facing the blank page, back to facing myself.

The next development, as I reconsider it, seems to involve someone else entirely, not me. Could I possibly be that man? I was, and I am. Will writing it down, writing it out, help? We shall see.

Return to the Chicago time.

One evening, Cordy came into my dressing room without knocking—her usual entrance—and said, "I'm ready with Juliet."

"Fine," I said.

"Can we have a session tomorrow?"

"You bet."

"Your suite?"

"Fine."

"Time?"

"Name it."

"Two-thirty?"

"I'll be waiting."

I was, but had forgotten that Pam was taping an interview with Studs Terkel in our suite at 2:30.

When Cordy arrived, I asked, "Can we go to your room?"

"Sure, but I have to go down and get the key."

"I'll come with you."

On the way back up in the elevator, she laughed and said, "Well, at least it'll be used for something."

I held my tongue.

Her room had the look and feel of a room you are just checking into. Barren. Unlived in.

"Good," she said, "it's still here."

She sat on the edge of the bed. I sat in the

armchair facing her.

"When you played Bianca last year," I began, "how aware were you of the five beats in every line, the iambic pentameter?"

"No. Should I have been?"

"Not while playing—but in rehearsal, yes. A large part of the magic of Shakespeare is in the rhythm. It has a subliminal effect on people, on audiences. In the same way that music does, whether it's classical or jazz. Now, I don't pretend to understand it all, but apparently it has something to do with the rhythm of the heartbeat. Most of Shakespeare—not all, but most of it—is written in that five-beat, iambic pentameter."

"I know," she said, "I've noticed it. Five beats. Ta-*da*-ta-*da*-ta-*da*-ta-*da*-ta-*da*."

"That's it. The beats aren't necessarily emphasized in the reading—no one wants to hear Hamlet say, 'To *be* or *not* to *be* that *is* the *question*.' But the rhythm is the glue that holds the whole miraculous design together—lines, whole speeches, scenes, even acts. And once in a while, you'll notice that the five beats are split up between two characters. For instance, in this opening *Romeo and Juliet* scene we're going to do, he sometimes has the first two beats and she has the last three. Or she has the first three and he has the last two. And that's important, too—because when you play a scene with one other person or two or three, all of you have to be aware of the flowing, continuing rhythm and that's what eventually catches the audience up. Someone once said it was like going to see and hear an effective evangelist. They work on the rhythms, too. And the Bible-thumpers. And that excites people, brings them to their feet, brings them sometimes to conversion on their knees."

"That's interesting," she said.

"I don't know if I ever told you this, but about ten years ago, Peter got us into a rehearsal at the National in London. Olivier working on Shylock. God Almighty! It was the second day—they were still holding books, and I noticed Olivier doing an odd thing. As he spoke, he marked the beat on his fingers like this—the thumb on his pinkie first, then the next finger and the next, then, the thumb on the forefinger, and finally, the forefinger on the thumb. See? Try it." She did. "Good. Now try it on one of Juliet's opening lines."

She did so, fingering the beats. "'*Mad*am, *I* am *here*. What *is* your *will?*' Hey, this is good!"

"The point is, darling, you somehow build in the rhythm working that way, and after a time, when it's there, you abandon it. Never forget that the whole thing is a poem. It's music. And the riding pulsating rhythm is what charges the audience up. God, I remember seeing Paul Schofield as Hamlet and when he got near to the end of that performance—

O. I die, Horatio!
The potent poison quite o'er crows my spirit.

CORDELIA?

I cannot live to hear the news from England,
But I do prophesy th' election lights
On Fortinbras. He has my dying voice.
So tell him, with th' occurrents, more and less,
Which have solicited—the rest is silence.

"I swear I thought I was going to have a heart attack. No wonder. That rhythm had been affecting my heartbeat for almost three hours."

Cordelia picked another line at random and tried the fingering trick again:

Give *me my* Romeo; and, *when* he *shall* die,
Take *him and* cut *him* out *in* little stars,
And he *will* make *the* face *of* heaven *so* fine,
That all *the* world *will* be *in* love *with* night
And pay *no* worship to *the* garish sun.

"I love that," she said. "It's how I feel about Tim."

"You're lucky," I said.

She was a true beauty, this daughter of mine. More beautiful than the other two. Perhaps because she resembled me the least. And when she spoke those last lines, she transcended even her own loveliness. I couldn't stop looking at her.

We got out our books—paperbacks of *The Pelican Shakespeare*.

"I've learned some of this," I said.

"I'm impressed."

"Not much."

"Well, then, I'm not much impressed."

"Their opening scene. He puts it in perfect rhyme. Did you notice?"

"Yes."

"So it's good to emphasize that a bit."

"I see."

"A daring spill, don't you think—considering the period?"

"I'll say."

"You'll notice there's no stage business indicated, but the scene is traditionally punctuated by various sorts of kisses. It's a sweet passage, really."

"You've never played Romeo, have you, Dad?"

"Only at the Academy," I said. "And now I'm too old. One of the troubles about acting is that by the time you're really able to play the great parts, you're too old for them."

"You're not too old for *anything,*" she said.

I touched her in gratitude. "Well, shall we have a go?"

"Sure."

"Remember, love, she's a girl of fourteen."

"I was once fourteen," she said. "Horrible time."

"Stand up."

She did.

Oh, Christ! I'm getting cold feet again. I don't believe I can go on with this. Maybe if I stop for a while.

(A couple of hours later. I have had a drink. Tell the truth! Isn't that the whole idea of this torturing exercise? Yes. All right, then. I have had *two* drinks.)
I moved to her as I began the scene:

If I profane with my unworthiest hand,
This holy shrine, the gentle sin is this:
My lips, two blushing pilgrims, ready stand
To smooth that rough touch with a tender kiss.

I leaned down and kissed her, gently. Now, I suppose that I had kissed my daughter thousands of times, but this time it was different. I was startled for an instant, then considered that, of course, this was not my daughter, this was Juliet. She pulled away slightly and continued the scene in a whisper. I noticed that she was marking the beat on her fingers.

Good pilgrim, you *do* wrong *your* hand *too* much,
Which man*nerly* devotion shows *in* this;
For saints *have* hands *that* pilgrims' hands *do* touch,
And palm *to* palm *is* holy palmers' kiss.

She held up the palm of her left hand and moved it toward me. I put the palm of my right hand on it.

She was trembling slightly as she moved in and kissed me.

It was a soft kiss and as she held it, she grasped my hand tightly. Admiring her invention, I went on quickly, eagerly:

Have not *saints* lips, *and* holy palmers too?

I was delighted when she picked up my tempo and shot back:

Ay, pilgrim, lips *that* they *must* use *in* prayer.

I moved still closer to her:

O, then, *dear* saint, *let* lips *do* what *hands* do!
They pray; *grant* thou, *lest* faith *turn* to despair.

She turned her head away as if to avoid another kiss.

Why had I never been aware of the exquisite view of her profile? Graceful and noble, ravishing.

Holding this position, she said:

Saints do *not* move, *though grant for* prayer's sake—

Still overwhelmed by the sight before me, I forgot my next line completely. She waited patiently,

CORDELIA?

remaining in character while I found my place in the book and read:

Then move *not* while *my* prayer's effect *I* take!

I moved around so that we were facing again. As I did so, I could not help appreciating the staging we had created and went on:

Thus *from my* lips, *by* thine *my* sin *is* purged—

She was looking down, shyly. I touched her chin and raised her head to mine. Her eyes seemed to open wider and wider as she said:

Then have *my* lips *the* sin *that* they *have* took.

I held the right side of her face in my hand and touched her lips with my thumb as I said:

Sin *from my* lips? *O* trespass sweetly urged!
Give *me my* sin again.

She smiled wickedly and completed the rhyme:

You kiss *by the* book.

She raised her Juliet face to mine, invitingly, tantalizingly.
We kissed. That is to say, Juliet and Romeo

115

kissed. Our bodies touched and strained toward one another. I became aware of the pressure of her firm breasts on my chest. She moved her head sensuously, dreamily from side to side and then—and then the world fell apart. I felt my tongue, like a hungry snake, thrust itself deep into her mouth. My book dropped to the floor, I heard hers fall as well. We embraced powerfully, and now her tongue found mine, caressed it feelingly, then made its way into *my* mouth. It was all unreal, hypnotic, and as the greatest kiss I have ever known continued, I felt my member swelling and stiffening. She must have felt it too, because she sent her middle toward it firmly, voraciously. Those lines of Marlowe's I had spoken a few seasons back ran through my head:

Sweet Helen, make me immortal with a kiss!
Her lips suck forth my soul; See where it flies.

I began returning to my senses, slowly. I was appalled. There was no use blinking the fact. We were no longer Romeo and Juliet. We were me—and my daughter.

We broke away from each other.

She fell back onto the bed, exhausted. Her skirt crept well above her knees.

"Wow!" she said, and covered her eyes with her arm. I stood looking down at her, and since I am setting all this down for a purpose, I will not deny to myself that at that moment, I considered bolting the door and lying down beside her. And I might have, if she had not prevented it by sitting up suddenly and laughing.

"So *that's* what you mean by 'let-go.'"

"Something like," I managed.

"And following instincts?"

"Yes."

"Well, I followed mine all right, didn't I?"

"Did you?"

"You bet."

She came to me and put her arms around me. I wanted to ask her to leave. I was frightened of the next half hour, but our coaching session had just begun.

"I think you *could* play Romeo, honestly. You're terrific!"

"You're not so bad yourself, kid."

"Dad . . ." she began tentatively.

"Yes?"

"Would you mind terribly if I begged off today?"

Oh, thank God! cried my brain. Go, go *now*. Please!

"The fact is," she continued, "it's been a great session—I think I got hold of something, and those beats and all and . . ."

"And . . . ?"

Her face was flushed.

"And . . . well . . . to tell you the truth . . ."

"Do."

"I want to go and find Tim and see if he's in the

mood. I know *I* am." She giggled. "I feel absolutely wanton. That scene turned me on like a three-alarmer!"

She had thrown me a cue for an old joke and I was relieved and grateful. Two reasons. One, I had changed my mind and did not want her to leave—not yet. Two, an exercise in levity would serve to defuse the disgraceful adventure.

I asked, "Did you ever hear this Ogden Nash?

> *The one-l lama*
> *He's a priest.*
> *The two-l llama,*
> *He's a beast.*
> *And I will bet*
> *A silk pajama*
> *There isn't any*
> *Three-l lllama.*

"No, never," she said and I went on.

"Well, when it was published Russel Crouse wrote him and said, 'You lose, Nash! How about a 'three-alarmer?'"

"I don't get it. Anyway, I'm off."

"I think I'll stay here until the interview's over. Is that all right?"

"Help yourself," she said.

She picked up her things swiftly, came to me, leaned forward and missed kissing my cheek by at least six inches. Then she ran—actually ran—out of

CORDELIA?

the room.

I bolted the door. I don't know why. I threw off my clothes, went into the bathroom and took a shower—hot to warm to cold to colder. I tried to look at myself in the mirror, but failed. I went back into the bedroom and dressed. I lay down on the bed, but only for a moment because it was still faintly redolent of the scent she had been wearing. Caleche, the same one Pam uses. The bed and the fragrance combined to cause an insane fantasy to form in my mind. What in God's name was happening to me? I looked at my watch. She had been gone now for about twenty minutes. I thought of what in all likelihood was happening in the room down the hall. In the movie of my mind I saw her and Tim in erotic action and I could not bear the picture or the thought, but neither would leave me. I lost control and began to weep, and continued to do so for some time. When finally I was able to stop I went back to the bathroom and doused my face with cold water. I still could not look at myself in the mirror. Then I tried to analyze my tears. What was I crying about? Remorse at the shocking thing I had done? Shame? What could Cordy be thinking? What if she told Tim? Her mother? Would they believe it was all part of the acting lesson? Not if she described what had happened with any degree of accuracy or detail. But surely, if she thought it was real, she would keep it to herself, wouldn't she? How could I be sure it wouldn't happen again? I heard myself say aloud,

"*Make* sure, goddamn it!" Should I tell Pam? Of course not. How could *she* understand when I don't understand myself? Just what I need, I thought—another guilt. So then I did what I had often done in crisis—I began talking to myself. A dialogue. A colloquy.

"*Jes-us* Christ, boy! You must be *sick*. Incest!

Hold it. Hold it. That was no incest. Nothing happened.

You call that *nothing?* You've never thrown a more lustful pass. And at your own daughter!

Carried away. The scene, I suppose.

Bullshit! The scene was over.

What if she'd responded? Really responded? You'd've wound up in the sack with her, with your daughter.

Don't keep saying that!

Why? Because it's true?

All right. So what? So I find my daughter attractive. Lots of fathers do."

I could see that I was getting nowhere. I wished Pam would call. I needed distraction.

What troubled me most was the fact that the outburst was not the end of it. I still felt an overwhelming desire to possess her in the way that that son of a bitch Tim was doing at that very moment. There was no point in denying it. Self-deception can be dangerous.

Then I began to think: Why Cordelia? Nothing like this had ever happened before. Not with Lynn,

CORDELIA?

not with Laurette, and we were always free and open with them. Nude bathing in the pool in California. Walking around the house bare-assed, all of us. What was it then? Something, anything to do with middle-age crisis?

Again and again the thought returned: Get help. Get professional help. But how the hell could I possibly reveal this horror to anyone, even to a doctor? Even to a doctor friend? *Especially* not to a doctor friend. No, I would deal with it myself. I was sweating profusely and needed a drink. My heartbeat rate had accelerated (dangerously?). I could *hear* the damned thing! I could not recall ever in life having been in such a state. I began to review it again, when fortunately for me, the phone rang. Pam.

"You finished?" she asked. "I am."

"—be right up."

Another dousing of my face with cold water. Fighting the mirror. Finally, I found the nerve and took a long look at that stranger reflected there. Did it show? Now I was trembling. A drink would stop that. Would it? Or would it make it worse?

"How'd it go?" I asked as I came into the suite.

She laughed. "Who was it said: 'I've never won an interview yet!'? We'll see. This one wasn't so bad actually. Studs is remarkable. Does great preparation. What about yours?"

"She's coming along. I showed her the Olivier finger thing."

"Oh, I *hate* that! I always get mixed up and need either one finger more or one finger less."

"Yes, well, of course, she's much brighter than you are."

"She certainly is. But has she got my spectacular animal magnetism?"

"No," I replied.

"Thank you."

"I want a drink," I said. "You?"

"Are you sure?" she inquired. "It's almost four-thirty."

"Don't *nag,* baby. I'm going to have a drink."

She looked at me, wondering what was the matter with me.

"All right," she said brightly. "I will, too."

"Are you sure?" I asked. "It's almost four-thirty."

"Don't *nag,* baby," she said. "I'm going to have a drink."

It felt good to laugh with her and drink with her and then instead of resting as we habitually did in the late afternoon, when we were in a play—to make love with her.

The tension was thus partially relieved until we got to the theater and I heard too much laughter from behind the closed door of Cordelia's dressing room.

CORDELIA?

The performance of *Private Lives* that night was strained and I found it difficult to concentrate. I don't suppose the audience noticed it, but Pam did.

"What *was* that tonight?" she asked at supper. "Something I did—or am doing?"

"No, no, just me. An off night. Started thinking about *Lear,* of all things."

"I wouldn't do that if I were you."

"Neither would I if I were me."

Even with the help of whiskey and milk, sleep would not come that night. I left the bedroom and paced about. I did half an hour of boring calisthenics. No use.

Then it hit me. And when I say hit, I mean that in the most literal sense. Let me attempt to describe it to myself. It was as though an implosion had occurred in the room. I felt intense pressure from the walls and the ceiling and the floor, all of which seemed to close in on me. I staggered, held on to an armchair and sat down, or rather, fell down into it.

I have never experienced a religious revelation or anything like it, but I understand now what is meant by "seeing the light." In a single moment it all seemed crystal clear. In one sense, I was grateful for the relief. But the negative aspect was excruciatingly painful. Torn. I was being torn apart. Or was I tearing *myself* apart?

What I suddenly believed—no—*knew* subconsciously, subliminally, atavistically, psychically and *positively* was that Cordelia was not my daughter.

After a time—I have no idea how long—I got up unsteadily and poured myself a drink.

My mind was racing. Almost nineteen years and out of them came flying sights and sounds, reactions, observations, remarks, jokes, all of which were germane to the subject.

It was a Niagara of remembrance that reinforced my knowledge.

Her inborn tendency constantly to pull away from the theater family. Her desire to become a veterinarian (stymied only by the accident of meeting the right man at the right time). I am not competent to think out the great heredity-environment question, but I am convinced that Cordelia possesses no talent for acting at all. In time she might become one of those actresses who do it all on will or nerve or persistence or beauty, but never with inspiration or natural talent. The fact is that her mother is one of those, as well. Pam once told me that she became interested in the theater at Wellesley because the drama society there was made up of men from Harvard and women from Wellesley, and she thought it would be an ideal way to "meet fellas." It was only later that she got caught up in it as a result of marrying an actor named Anthony Mills who got her a job in summer stock. Then came the competitive process and trying to match him. (He was a supremely gifted young actor who did it all effortlessly. I have always admired him.) Pam told me that it was the strain caused by her inability to keep up with him that in time resulted in the dissolution of their marriage. But she was (is) enormously intelligent and determined. Moreover, she is the hardest-working actress I know. Her methodology is a model. No detail escapes her attention. She coaches constantly and takes part in workshops. She has studied at the Actors' Studio with Strasberg, with Uta Hagen at Hagen/Berghof, with Stella Adler. She takes singing lessons and dancing lessons, and tends to her person with dedication and energy. So she has made herself into a competent, reliable, dependable actress and when she has the luck of a part—scores. But she is not a born actress, she is a manufactured one. The kind I am trying to turn Cordelia into by coaching. (And that, by the way, I have considered, will have to come to a halt. I will get her someone else, make some excuse. I don't want to find myself alone in a room with her again. Ever.)

I was: one, in turmoil; two, relieved.

I thought of her again and again, feeling freer now to exercise my fantasies without shame or self-disgust. Again my skin tingled, my temperature rose, my middle came alive.

I conjured up an extreme close-up of her. She smiled at me; I smiled back at the pellucid apparition. Of course, she did not resemble me at all, in spite of what Peter and others have said from time to time. No. She looks exactly like her *mother*. In fact, more and more as the years go by.

Dramatically unstrung and disquieted as I was by my newfound conviction, it was balanced by my utter relief in learning that I was not an incestuous father.

However, by the time the first streaks of light appeared over Lake Michigan, my world began collapsing and sickening self-doubt set in. In the light of day, confidence in my supposition began to fade, to melt in the powerful rays of the morning sun.

Could it be that I had imaginatively created this entire postulation simply as a cop-out? As a way of getting myself off a near-criminal hook? As a desperate means of crawling out of a morass of self-revulsion? Playing judge and jury and acquitting myself on the flimsiest alibi?

"Dr. Herter, please. Alan Standish calling."

"He's on the other line, Mr. Standish, can you hold?"

"I'm calling from Chicago."

"Oh. Well, let me let him know you're on."

I waited, wondering whether or not I could pull this off, make it sound convincing. I reminded myself that I was a professional actor. So? So, act!

"Alan! How are you?"

"Fine, Fred. We're all fine, it's just that I have a question."

"Shoot."

"Well, you may not believe this, but I'm writing a play."

"Good." He sounded as though he couldn't care less.

"Well, it's not good yet, but I hope it will be."

"And the question?" He was hurrying me along.

"Well, the question is this: Is it possible—I need it for a turn in the plot—is it possible to tell for certain if a man, if a certain man is the father of a certain child? I mean, is there some sort of a blood test or something of the kind that—"

He interrupted. "Do you mean to tell me you called me from Chicago for this?"

"Why, yes."

"I just got off a three-way telephone consultation conference for this, you dolt. I thought someone was ill, or an accident . . . or . . ."

"I'm sorry, Fred," I said, "should I call you back?"

"No, no, now that you're here . . . what was it again?"

"Well, this man, in my play, suspects that a child of his—a son—is not his. Can he prove it, one way or the other?"

"Complicated. It comes up in court a good deal, paternity suits, and so on. The answer seems to be— you can tell if he definitely is not—but there is no way of telling definitely if he *is*."

"Well, *not* is good enough for my purpose, thanks. How's the missus?"

"She's fine, I wish you were."

"Me?"

"You sound distracted."

"Oh, well, you know—Chicago. Thanks a lot."

"Love to Pam."

"Right."

"Bye."

"Goodbye."

What had he meant "distracted"? Could he guess something? The writing-a-play thing didn't sound convincing at all. Well, what the hell.

"Hello?"

"It's Hank, Alan."

"Oh, thanks, Hank, thanks for calling back."

"Are you all right?"

"Fine."

"Everyone?"

"Sure. I just need a piece of information."

"What is it?"

"It's about Cordy—but listen, Hank, it's a secret, a surprise I'm planning for her, a birthday thing. What's her blood type? Do you know?"

"What on earth's the matter with you, Alan? Do you think I carry all my patients' blood types around in my head, for God's sake?"

"No, of course not, but haven't you got the information there, somewhere?"

"Certainly, but—listen, do you need it right now? This minute?"

"Yes, I do."

"All right. Hang on."

CORDELIA?

Why were all the doctors so testy? They were not only doctors, they were friends. Was there something about my controlled hysteria that communicated itself and made them nervous? Who was it said, "A nervous person is a person who makes other persons nervous"? Hank returned.

"It's AB."

"AB?"

"Right."

"Thanks a lot."

"Honestly, you *people!*"

He hung up without saying goodbye and before I had a chance to do so.

I immediately got out that medicard that Fred makes everyone in the family carry and found that my blood type was O.

Back to Fred. This time I did not ask to speak to him but simply left word with his secretary asking him to call me back at his convenience.

"What is it now?" he asked, still cross.

"Suppose the father's type O, and the son—the son's—is AB, could the father be the father?"

"Yes, of course, and the son could be the son."

"Oh."

He sensed the disappointment in my voice and asked, "What's the matter? If you're writing a play, can't you make it anything you like?"

"Certainly."

"Then what's the problem?"

"No problem. Who said there was a problem?"

He spoke seriously. "What *is* all this, Alan? Are you really writing a play?"

"Certainly."

"You're touring *Private Lives,* planning *King Lear and* writing a play? All at the same time?"

"Sure, why not?"

"Are you crazy?"

"Yes."

"You're back on the overdoing again. Pam's worried about you."

"Bye, Fred."

Where was I? Nowhere, but one thing I had learned from the last conversation with Fred. I had to be more careful—much more careful with all this detecting. I was a rank amateur and was sure to make a serious blunder if I didn't proceed with more caution.

Now began a week of consulting calendars and diaries and old programs and correspondence. Arithmetic has never been a strong point of mine, so it took time. Pam had said she *knew* Cordelia was conceived on the opening night of the 1961 *Lear,* but could *I* be sure of that? Counting backward from Cordelia's birthday, March 3, 1962, the impregnation would have had to be on or about June 3—give or take a few days or even a week. Was I doing this right?

June 4, 1961 was the opening date of *Lear*

CORDELIA?

all right, but what else was going on around that time?

My own rare infidelities were usually confined to idle time, certainly never during rehearsals or runs or tours. Was Pam's pattern the same?

Shortly after we were married, we decided that so long as extramarital activity was casual and short-lived and infrequent, we would treat it naturally. Another rule was—we would not tell about it unless specifically asked, and then we would tell the truth.

She had had occasion to ask me only twice. Once she was right; another time, all wrong.

I had never asked her, although on occasion I had suspected some goings-on, usually with much younger men. Across our years we found that an open account of our respective social histories often proved to be a turn-on, an aphrodisiac.

I formulated a plan.

From Chicago we went to Los Angeles, but had to lay off one whole week because of a booking problem.

Cordy and Tim went to San Francisco for the week. Pam and I chose Santa Barbara where we had spent our honeymoon. We tried to get the same bungalow but were told that it was unavailable. No matter.

When we arrived, however, the manager (a fan)

told us that he had explained the situation to the occupants of our old bungalow and that they had volunteered to move out and leave it to us. So the week began well.

We walked long distances, read, studied some *Lear*—but mainly we made love. The tour had been, thus far, exhausting. It is a well-known theater rule that to play comedy you need not only energy, but the *cream* of your energy.

I awakened her early one morning with our most tender intimate, special, private kiss. She purred and moved and undulated, and it was the beginning of a memorable hour.

Afterward I said, "I don't understand how either of us ever wanted to go off with anyone else. We seem so *right* together. A fact, in fact."

"Perfect," she said.

"Restless, do you suppose? Greener grass?"

"No idea."

"The truth is," I said, proceeding in a gingerly, careful way—"the truth is, all of mine have been during your pregnancies."

"Not *all*," she said, opening one eye.

"And what about yours?" I asked. "During *my* pregnancies?"

"Oh, don't ask me to remember—there were so *many!* Hundreds."

I slapped her bottom lightly.

"Come on," I urged.

"Where?"

CORDELIA?

"Tell me the first one ever, and I'll tell you mine."

"You don't have to, I know it."

The atmosphere between us was beginning to be charged.

I held her close, and persisted. "Tell me. Come on, tell me."

"You'll die," she said.

"I'm ready."

"All right. Remember when I was up for the *Mary, Mary* replacement and I kept auditioning and auditioning?"

"Yes."

"And you had to go to London for a week for that BBC thing?"

"Yes."

"And you asked Lenny to sort of take care of me and take me to dinner and the theater so that I wouldn't get too lonely?"

"Of course." I kissed her ear.

"Well, he did."

"Did what?"

"Take care of me."

I let go of her abruptly and sat up. "You really are putting me on now, aren't you? Lenny's an angel—and as gay as a grig."

"He wasn't *that* week," she said in her irritating singsong.

I got out of bed slowly and moved around to the front of it.

"You're not telling me that Lenny . . . we'd been

married—what?—how long?"

"Two and a half years, and I'll admit . . . well, remember it was our first separation and I was getting a little antsy, so he didn't face much resistance."

For some reason I picked up my dressing gown and put it on.

Pam continued. "Another explanation might have been that I knew . . . I just *knew* what would happen in London when you made contact with your leading lady—after all, they don't call her 'The British Open' for nothing . . . I notice you don't say no."

"No."

"No, what? No, no, or no, yes?"

"It was nothing."

"I'm delighted to hear it."

We got dressed and went for a walk.

How we got hooked on the tube that night, I can't explain. The champagne, I expect, but we sat there through the 11:00 news and Johnny Carson and Tom Snyder and *The Maltese Falcon* right to the end. 4:10 A.M. An unreal time, especially in Santa Barbara.

We drank milk.

I asked, "How well do you remember sixty-one up there in Stratford?"

"Pretty well.

CORDELIA?

*The scary year
Of the terrible Lear,*

she recited.

"Remember the boy who played the Fool so well? A Canadian kid with blue, blue eyes."

"Of course. Jeff Harley. He was *excellent.*"

I moved to her, knelt before her and put my forehead between her breasts.

"I got the feeling he had the flaming hots for you."

"He did," she said, kissing my ear.

"And you for him?"

"Well, not *flaming,* no." I felt her tongue enter my ear.

"But something?"

"I suppose you could call it that. Something. God, you were beastly to me on that show."

"Because you were so terrible as Regan."

I reached in and cupped her breast with my right hand.

"So were you."

"Not as Regan, I wasn't."

"No, as Lear you were."

She spread her knees and drew me closer. "You yelled at me all the time, you bully bastard."

She was holding the back of my neck and caressing it in the magical way she had discovered long ago. We kissed.

"I was yelling at *myself,* baby. You know that."

"I know it now. I didn't know it then. You

humiliated me, you stinkin' rotten thing. I thought I was back with Tony again." She reached down, found me, touched me. "So it was revenge, mostly. I didn't enjoy it much. He really was *too* young."

"And too blond."

"Yeah."

"And too blue-eyed."

"No," she said, "he wasn't blue-eyed."

"Yes, he was," I insisted, as my hand made its way to her. "Blue-eyed," I whispered, "without a doubt . . . just like Cordy—"

And all at once I was on my back on the floor. She had thrust me off violently and now was kicking me—in my sides, in my thighs and trying for my head. For half a minute or so, I was too startled to move. Then I tried to get up but she pushed me down again, knelt down beside me and began to pummel me with her fists. I jumped up now, terrified, prepared to defend myself even if it meant knocking her cold, but the attack was over, apparently. She had flung herself onto the sofa, sobbing hysterically. I was not sure why. I had several ideas, but not one.

She stopped crying as abruptly as she had begun, stood up, looked at me, and said, "You pig! How *dare* you! This is it, you crafty bastard. I'm *through* with you! This is the absolute *end*—right now!" She stormed into the bedroom and began to dress. I followed her.

"What *is* all this?"

"Get out of here! I'm warning you, Alan. Leave

me alone. I'm liable to do *anything!*"

"Where do you think you're going. It's almost five."

"I'll hit the road," she said. "I'm sure I'll find a few blue-eyed truck drivers who'll give me a ride—*if* you know what I mean."

"Come on, Pam—reason, huh?"

"Right," she said. "Reason."

She sat down, crossed her legs. "You are a tricky, devious, crooked, lying lousebub. For some insane, demented, paranoid, neurotic reason, you think Cordy is not yours. Well, she *is,* my boy—for better or worse—she is. But that sick thought, having crossed your diseased mind, there is no future for us ever ever ever ever—"

"Will you *stop?*" I shouted, caught out and scared, "talk about paranoid! *What* in the name of sweet Jesus ever gave you the idea that I—why, that's the goddamndest—"

"You are giving, my boy—my *ex*-boy—one of your worst performances ever. You are as transparent to me as a scrim. I see right through you—I always have. You never deceived me—not once. That asinine rule, 'we never tell until we're asked and then we tell the truth.' The truth! You don't know the *meaning* of the word! When I *knew* you were balling Angela's theater maid, for Christ's sake, and I asked you, you slapped me! And it was true and I knew it and you knew I knew it! What a farce!"

"Pam," I said as quietly as I could, "whatever happens, happens. If you really want to leave, I won't stop you or try—but you are dead wrong" (like hell) "I can't imagine what set you off" (liar)—

"Blue eyes—you're so goddamn worried about blue eyes, as if that would mean anything. Jesus! On top of everything else you're *ignorant!* Naive."

"Pam, listen," I said, and went to her. She got up and whacked the side of my head. I have never been struck more powerfully, not even when I was boxing at Amherst. I felt like a comic-strip character as I staggered back among the stars in my head. It took me a few minutes to recover and by the time I did she had left.

I got dressed and went looking for her. The night clerk said he had not seen her. I thought she might have checked into another room, but no. I went out to the parking lot and, as I might have known, the car was gone.

I phoned the Beverly Hills Hotel and asked the desk clerk to inform me if she turned up there.

"I'll make it worth your while," I said, "if you keep it confidential."

"My lips are sealed, Mr. Standish," he said. "I hope everything turns out all right."

I began to pack. Twenty minutes later the phone rang. On my way to answer it, I glanced at my watch. No way she could have got there, was there? Plane? I was making no sense. "Yes?"

"Mr. Standish?"

"Yes?"

"This is Ralph at the Beverly Hills?"

"Yes."

"I just heard from her. Your wife."

"Where is she?"

"I don't know. She wouldn't say but she wanted to make sure we could put her up when she got here. I told her the suite we've got reserved for you won't be ready—but we'll find something. She said just a single room. Is that all right?"

"For now, yes. Thanks a lot. And tell Hollis, or leave a note, I'll want a suite later today—say about noon."

"Got it. And listen, Mr. Standish, you don't have to make it worth my while. Glad to do it. You know, I used to be in the business myself. Mostly for George Abbott. *Pajama Game. Damn Yankees. Fiorello.* Boy! Some days."

"Thanks again."

Thirteen

The next four weeks are beyond my powers of description.

Pam refused to speak to me under any circumstances or for any reason. When our bungalow suite was ready she stayed on in her dinky single and wrote me a note:

> Give up that bungalow and take a room like mine. Tell Wally I want a complete dress rehearsal on Monday afternoon. Sound, lights, music. I hope you are in pain.

The dress rehearsal was a nightmare. Daymare? *Private Lives* may be the most romantic comedy in the English language. Pam, the perfect professional, played beautifully—better than ever before. Probably because she didn't give a damn about me or about what I thought. She didn't hold back anything in any of the intimate, physical love scenes and for some reason looked more alluring than I had ever seen her.

I tried to talk to her several times but it was no use. Between Acts II and III, Estelle, her maid, brought me another note.

> The Wilders are picking me up and taking me to dinner. Please stay away. I have told them you are not free—business. Do not have dinner at La Scala. I thought you were unforgivably slow in Act I today.

After the dress, she left the theater with the Wilders. She had made a movie four years earlier with Billy and they had remained close friends.

I took Tim and Cordy to Yamato because Cordy is a Japanese food buff. Over sake martinis I explained the situation to them as best I could.

"But what was it all about?" Cordy asked.

"Please don't ask, Cordy. It's too personal."

"Is there anything *I* can do?" asked Tim.

"No, but there's quite a lot you can *not* do."

"Such as?"

"Don't pry, don't guess, don't discuss it with anyone. I know this town. Don't try peacemaking, don't let it affect your performances. Now. Let's eat everything on the goddamn menu."

I kept studying Cordelia throughout the long meal. What if I were wrong? Where would this

CORDELIA?

damned obsession lead?

We opened at the Ahmanson triumphantly, even though the theater was too large for our play. Still, a big theater means a big audience which means big laughs and in a comedy, nothing matters more.

Pam and I exchanged letters almost daily. It was a surreal situation.

Dear Wife,

You have misread me, misunderstood me, misinterpreted me, and are causing agony to yourself and to me.

This absence of real communication will serve only to exacerbate the matter.

These silly back and forth notes are idiotic and you know it. Please let us meet and discuss everything.

I thought you played the play better last night than ever before, and you looked fantastic.

Please!

A.

Her reply:

Sir:

If I believed I could contain my fury I would gladly meet with you but I would doubtless wind up striking you again and I did not find it enjoyable.

Misread, misunderstood, misinterpreted my foot! For better or worse I know you and your guile and your methods.

You are a superlative actor—because you convey what your character is thinking and feeling no matter what he is doing or saying. So the other night it was your inestimable talent that betrayed you. Never mind that you were nuzzling me and touching me and beginning your prodigious, ever-surprising foreplay—what was going on in your mind became increasingly clear. So foul a suggestion that I cannot bear to dignify it by setting it down here on the page.

Of course I realize what complications this cleavage will bring about for both of us—but these will have to be sorted out in time one way or another.

The principal one is, needless to say, the Stratford season.

My first impulse is to chuck it, and perhaps it will be my last as well. I am still thinking it over.

But no—I cannot face a face-to-face. The thought of it makes me ill.

                                        Pamela

The formality of the signature disturbed me more

than anything. I had not called her Pamela in years. At the very beginning, yes, but certainly not after we were married. Was she returning us to our premarital status? The idea of calling off the Stratford season was unthinkable, yet I got from her letter the sense that she was prepared to walk. It would not wreck the season, but it certainly would put one hell of a crimp in it. I thought long and hard about my next move in this delicate, complex chess game.

Dear Pam (not Pamela, for God's sake!),

I, too, have been agonizing about Stratford.

If ever there was a time for grace under pressure, this is it—for both of us.

Certainly cancellation is a possibility. It would mean a frightful upheaval for Peter and the management and the casts and added expense that might bankrupt the whole Stratford Festival. (Lawsuits? Damages?) But they could, I suppose, replace us all or swiftly put together a completely different season.

Too bad. We have an enormous investment of time and effort in *Private Lives*—and doubtless the kids will be bitterly disappointed—but they are young and there will be other opportunities.

One important point: If we *are* going to cancel—we should in good conscience do it soon. To delay it would be wicked and unprofessional.

I shall be guided entirely by you in this—your wishes and your convenience.

Let me know.

Alan Standish

Somewhere in here I was astonished one night to see her leave the theater with Anthony Mills, her first husband. Where in hell did he spring from? Did he live out here? Was he making a movie? What was going on?

My dear Alan Standish,

That was just about the most comical letter you have ever written. And you have written some doozies!

Your schemingness (is that a word?) is so obvious that it is like someone playing a tender love scene with his fly open! I read your letter to Tony and he laughed, too. We agreed that you were saying exactly the opposite of what you meant in an effort to get me to do what you want.

About Tony. Strange—is it not?—that in this crisis (the worst I have ever known in all my life) the only one I could think of to talk to was Tony. I called him and he flew out at once. He has been a tower of strength and kind and understanding and supporting and dear—all the things he was not when we were married! Needless to say I am seeing a lot of him and who knows . . . ? (Would you consider him for Gloucester in *Lear* if he can get free and if, if, if?)

F.Y.I. I have *not* told him about Santa Barbara. I do not see how I could. That is between you and me—or perhaps between you and you. I told him only that we have had a basic, serious, irreconcilable quarrel and that in all probability our marriage is over.

I am in such a muddle and disturbed state that I would not trust my judgment about anything, so I have decided to let Tony make the decision for me. As soon as he lets me know I shall let you know.

I agree with you that there should be no undue delay. Tony agrees as well. So.

Pamela

That is the note Estelle handed me after the Wednesday matinee. It threw me. *Tony* for the love of God! How the hell did *he* get back into the act? I went out and walked for three hours, stopping only at the sushi bar of Mishimoto in Japantown to order food which I could not eat. What was most irritating of all was the realization that I had lost my power of conning her. Next, that I (and work and career) appeared to be at her mercy—and Tony's.

My dear Mrs. Standish (and don't you forget it!),

I trust that you and Tony will enjoy this letter. I shall do my best to make it even more entertaining than my last. I await your/Tony's decision with interest but I feel that I should make certain stipulations. For one thing, in the unlikely event that you/Tony decide to go forward, this idiot farce of not speaking will have to come to an end. I have no intention of going through a five-week rehearsal schedule and a ten-week season in the lunatic way you have persisted in pursuing here.

As to Tony's possible involvement—you know that I think most highly of his abilities, but the casting from here on in is in Peter's hands and I advise Tony if he is interested to contact Peter or have his agent do so.

Finally, if we do go to Stratford, we must make at least a show of living together. Whether we do or not *actually* I leave to you—but the front matters, at least to me.

Your turn.

A.S.

Her reply came within an hour.

Tony advises me—and strongly—to honor my commitment to Peter and to Stratford in spite of you.

Therefore I am prepared to do so.

About communication. Of course I am not

such a fool (no matter what *you* think) as to be unaware of the necessity of work contact. What I will not do is resume any personal relationship *whatsoever*.

About Stratford living arrangements. We must get them to rent the Findlay house for us. I know that Cordy and Tim will want to be off by themselves so we will have the whole house. It has five bedrooms. I shall need one for Estelle and if Tony is with us—one for him. That would leave one extra for you should you decide to use it. Tony's possible involvement is still vague.

I am planning to fly back to New York the Sunday after we close here. I presume you are going directly to Stratford. Let me know if there is anything you want me to bring or send from the apartment.

Mauvais voyage.

                              Pamela

In reply to this I wrote:

Dearest Pam,

I have begged for your understanding, I have grovelled. If you want more begging and grovelling, I am prepared to supply it. In time you will see how wrong you are about all this and what a cruel waste it has been. Speaking of transparency and schemingness (no, there *is* no such word) and deviousness and craftiness—you, dear girl, are right up there with the rest of us.

Do you think for one female hysterical moment that I believe all that horseshit about how you are going to let Tony make the decision? You wouldn't let that popinjay decide what wine to have at one of your charming little tête-à-tête dinners for Christ's sake! You told me once that he was incapable of putting his mind on any subject with the exception of himself. You told me that you considered him a peacock with talent but no brains.

You brought him out here in order to burn my ass—and you succeeded, you will be pleased to learn. (Wait till I show you the bill from the Burn Center at the Cedars of Lebanon!)

And do you honestly believe for even one fleeting, lunatic instant that I would live in a house with you and him or that *you* would?

No, baby, it's all high and mighty counterpunching and it's annoying rather than truly damaging.

In any case, all this is academic because I have called Peter and told him that he would probably be hearing from Tony or Tony's agent—and that in spite of the fact that I think he (Tony, not his agent) would make a tremendous Gloucester and that he might just accept the role to hang around you in the hope of, I told Peter that I did not want Tony in the company and that if by any chance he turned up in Stratford I would leave. So I expect Peter will know what to do.

Aside from which, I may or may not go directly to Stratford. I may go to New York to *our* apartment—not *the* apartment, *our* apartment. So if you want anything brought or sent, let me know.

Dearest, you are driving me mad. I love you with all my heart and body and spirit and being and past and present and future and shall continue to do so until the day I die.

Allie

I read it over a few times, then put a match to it and watched it disappear in the flame.

Fourteen

I did go directly to Stratford via Toronto and a damned good thing I did, too, because Peter met me at the airport with a body blow.

"Brace yourself," he said as we shook hands. "Lynn is out."

"What're you talking about?"

"—all happened today. She tried to reach you and when she couldn't, she called me."

"But why? What happened?"

"Look, Alan, I don't want to get into this, it's none of my business, but apparently it's something to do with the situation between you and Pam. I understand Lynn had a rouser with her mother about it and says that in the circumstances she doesn't want to be around. She says the strain would make it impossible for her to function and what's more that it would probably ruin her health."

"I'll call her," I said.

"All right. But I'm starting to audition girls in the morning."

It took me hours but I finally tracked Lynn down at a girlfriend's apartment in New York.

"Oh, Daddy! I'm *so* glad to hear from you. Are you all right?"

"Considering everything, yes," I said. "But what's this about you quitting?"

There was a long pause.

"Lynn?" I asked.

"Wait a minute." Another pause, then, "Daddy, I can't talk to you from here. Give me your number. I'll go out and call you from the street."

"Oh, God," I said, "don't do that! The Village at three in the morning? The street?"

"Well, tomorrow, then."

"But let me ask you. Just say yes or no, is there any chance I can get you to change your mind?"

"No."

"Are you sure?"

"Yes."

"All right, then. Call me in the morning, any time."

At 9:00 A.M. I called Pam and woke her up. In her sleepiness she forgot that we were not speaking.

"Yah?" she croaked.

"It's me, Pam."

"Who?"
"Alan."
"What time is it, f'God's sake?"
"About nine."
"God! Hold on." A noisy pause. "What's the matter?"
"We've got to talk."
"What? Wait. Who did you say this is?"
"Alan. Alan Standish. Your husband. We've got to talk."
Now she came to, more or less. "How can we talk?" she asked. "We're not speaking."
Before I could reply she laughed at her odd locution. A perfect example of her antic sense of humor.
"Where are you?" she asked.
"Stratford."
"What are you doing up *there?*"
"At this point, I'm not sure."
"What time is it?"
"Nine."
"Call me later. In an hour. I can't think or talk or anything."
"It's important, Pam."
She hung up.
Then Lynn phoned. I stayed on with her for almost an hour. She went through the complete cycle of human emotion: fury, tears, anxiety, worry, laughter, ridicule, the lot. I could not persuade her, but she persuaded *me* that the situation would indeed be untenable for her. I gave up.

Then she said, "But if you want me to come up and be with you for a while, I'll leave right now. I love you, Daddy."

I found it difficult to speak. My throat was in a clutch. "No, no, I'll be all right," I said.

At ten, I tried Pam again. This time she was awake and hostile.

"I thought we had an understanding, Alan," she said.

"This is business."

"Go on."

"It's about Lynn, of course."

"That silly little bitch? I suppose she told you I slapped her. Well, I'm not sorry."

"You did *what?*"

"She had no right to talk to me the way she did. It's none of her business."

"You're getting to be quite a slapper, ol' girl. You'd better pull yourself together. One of these days you'll get slapped back."

"Any more sage advice?"

"Not on the phone, no. But we've got to get together and talk."

"Where are you?"

"Stratford."

"Listen, did we talk earlier? I mean, before?"

"Yes."

"What time?"

"About nine."

"And what did I say?"

"You told me to call you at ten."

"Oh. But if you're up there, how can we meet?"

"I'll come down. Or you could come up. You're due here in three days anyway."

"Can't it wait?"

"No."

"All right, then. Come down."

I did not say what I wanted to say. Instead, I said, "See you at about five."

"All right."

She hung up before I could say goodbye.

Fifteen

The minute I entered the apartment I knew that something about the situation had changed. The place was beautifully scented. Had she done it, or had Conchita, our maid? The hi-fi was on playing a Fats Waller album—one of my favorites. Conchita wouldn't have put *that* on. Then Pam came in wearing a short, cotton skirt and a near-transparent blouse and no bra. She had on no makeup of any kind which she knows is my favorite look. Her hair was tied back with a bright yellow ribbon. She sat down at once and crossed her legs tantalizingly.

"How's Stratford?" she asked.

"Chaotic. You can imagine."

I was trying to think quickly. Did all this signify a hint at reconciliation? Or was it part of a monumental tease? I looked at her legs. She uncrossed them.

"Let's get one thing out of the way first," she said. "I'm sorry I slapped Lynn. And for that matter, I'm sorry I slapped you."

"That was more than a slap," I said. "You damn near took my head off."

"Not that the two of you didn't deserve it, but I don't like being out of control."

"What was it with Lynn?"

"She wanted to know why I'd come home alone, so I told her."

I was astonished. "Not about Santa Barbara!"

"Of course."

"You couldn't have made up something?"

"Why should I?"

"Because this is truly fruity. You tell her what *you* think *I* thought. Where's the sense?"

"No—what I *know* you thought."

"And what did she say?"

"Something that made me slap her."

"What?"

"She said she thought I was crazy."

"She's wrong about that."

"Thank you."

"And she shouldn't have said it. I'll speak to her."

"But before we got to *that* she lectured me as though *I* was *her* daughter."

"I know. She does that with me sometimes. Mother to son."

"She'll calm down."

"And will *you?*"

"Look at me. Calm as a daisy."

CORDELIA?

"The last letter I wrote to you—boy, wasn't *that* a routine from *Alice in Wonderland,* those letters?"

"I sort of enjoyed them."

"Yours or mine?"

"Both."

"As I was saying, the last one I wrote I didn't send—I burned it."

"Why did you do that?"

"It was no good."

"Oh."

"Some of it was, though—the part where I said: 'Dearest, darling Pam, my wife, my life—you are driving me mad. And I miss you to a point of terror. And I love you with all my heart and body and soul and spirit and past, present, and future. I love you more every day and miss you more every night and will continue to do so for the rest of my life no matter what or where or...'"

By this time she was in tears. I moved to her, slowly and gently.

She looked up. "Don't come near me," she said.

I went to the bar and made two martinis. We said nothing more until we had consumed them.

I asked, "Were you surprised when she quit?"

"What?"

"When she quit. Did she say she was going to or—"

"What are you talking about?"

"About Lynn. Quitting Stratford."

This brought her to her feet.

"Look here you rogue, if this is another one of

your goddam schemes—"

"Jesus, Pam! Will you come off it? I heard about it from Peter when I got off the plane. She couldn't reach me so she called him."

"Quit, why?"

"Because of us—the situation. She said she didn't think she could handle it—you know, the strain. And I see her point."

"Well, if the other two can, she can."

"No use, Pam. I tried for an hour almost."

"Give me another drink," she said.

As I prepared two more, I said, "The other two. Cordy's safe. She's coming on account of Tim. But Laurette . . ."

"She wants the part," said Pam. "She doesn't give a damn about us or what we do or don't do."

"I'm not so sure."

Silence again as we drank. Two drinks—especially martinis—invariably loosen her up making her especially loquacious and often imaginative.

"Take me to dinner," she said suddenly. "I've got a flash but it needs some refining. I mean a real posh New York dinner. Grenooly or Le Cirque or like that."

"It's late—do you think we can get in?"

"Mention my name," she said airily.

As she started out of the room I took a breath and asked, "What about Tony?"

"He's gone. You won't believe this, but that crude oaf made a lunging pass at me—right here in this room. I slapped *him,* too, the poltroon."

I began to laugh and could not stop and she began

CORDELIA?

to laugh and we got to laughing together and wound up in each other's arms. I was about to kiss her—or try—when she said, "Don't get any ideas, my boy. Come on. I'm hungry."

Over a splendid meal at La Grenouille, she outlined her scheme. (We had had a third martini and were sharing a bottle of Cristal champagne. I knew we would be spending the night together.)

"The idea is this," she said. "We've got to outsmart the little monster."

"Zzz," I said.

"What?"

"Monster*s*. Because don't be too sure about Laurette."

"All right," she said. "Monster*zzz*. We call a family confab. Right away. Tomorrow. At the apartment. We sit together—you and I—on the sofa, and hold hands—and we tell them that yes, we *did* have a row—but that it was all a big misunderstanding and that it's all made up and we're happily rec—rec—what's the damn word?"

"Wrecked?" I suggested.

"Come on," she said. "Help me!"

"Reconciled."

"Reconciled."

"You're welcome."

"And so—all systems go, and on as before. Then, once we're up there, we—I mean you and I—simply carry out the plan we agreed on and who's to know?"

"—won't work."

"We'll *make* it work. Have picnics and dinners

163

and act. We're actors aren't we? So let's act."

"Let me think about it."

After lemon soufflé and coffee and brandy, we walked up Fifth Avenue in the sweet spring evening and were recognized four times.

When we reached the canopy of 845 I started into the lobby with her. She stopped and said, "Thank you for dinner. It was surpassing. Call me in the morning, O.K.? Not too early."

"What're you talking about, Pam? That's my apartment up there as much as it is yours."

"I know, but I am just a trifle looped, Alan, and nervous—and confused—and I don't want to take any chances."

"But where do you expect me to go?"

"How about the Athletic Club?"

"What if they don't have a room?"

"The Algonquin?"

"All right," I said, as calmly as I could. "I'll just come up and get a change of clothes and a razor."

"Fine," she said, "I'll wait here."

She moved into the lobby and sat down.

I spent a fitful night at the club and phoned her at 8:00 A.M. She was furious.

"Do you know what time it is!" she yelled.

"Of course I do," I yelled back. "It's eight A.M., and if we're going to arrange our happy family meeting we've got to get the hell going. I've got to be back in Stratford tonight."

"Goddam it!" she said and slammed down the phone.

She had once heard somewhere that British upper-class beauties preserve their smashing looks by making it a rule never to be awakened artificially, but always to sleep out sleep.

I decided on one of our favorite group rituals—a picnic lunch in Central Park. There was a spot not far from the apartment's entrance that all of us favored.

Cordelia flatly refused to come without Tim and I had to agree.

Laurette seemed delighted.

Lynn was intransigent and suspicious and it was necessary for me to meet with her and to use all of my persuasive powers to get her to change her mind.

I went up to William Poll's and bought six of his finest picnic baskets, then to Sherry-Lehmann for wine, and made my way to the appointed spot. Surprisingly, everyone was on time. A good omen? We sat on the blankets that Pam had brought and began.

"Listen kids," I said. "You know that there have never been any secrets in this family—maybe there should have been . . ." I waited for the laugh which did not come. "Anyway, I think you all know that mother and I had a disagreement—well, a serious quarrel, actually, in California."

"It was my fault," said Pam gamely, taking my hand.

"Yes, it was," I said.

She squeezed my hand so hard that I winced. Powerful woman.

She said, "We were both tired from the tour and what with one thing and another—"

"Anyway," I continued, "when Lynnie heard about it she got all upset."

"We *all* did, Dad," said Laurette.

"I know, but Lynnie decided not to go to Stratford with us."

Cordelia closed her eyes and mumbled something to herself.

"What did you say?" asked Lynn.

"Nothing, dear. Nothing. You know me. I talk to myself."

"May I go on?" I asked.

"Please do," said Pam.

"From her point of view—Lynnie's—she was quite right and both Mother and I respected it. You can imagine what a blow it was to Peter and to the management—I mean to say, without Lynnie, the whole concept was wrecked."

"Silly, anyway," said Lynn. "A gimmick. Who cares?"

"You're so *wrong,* Lynnie!" said Cordelia. "It's a first."

We all worked on her but the concerted effort served only to reinforce her obstinacy.

"It's no use," she said. "I'm not going. Anyway, I've signed up for summer classes at A.B.T."

"When?" asked Pam.

"This morning."

"Why?" I asked. "You knew we were meeting. Couldn't you have waited?"

"I didn't want to be pressured. Anyway, as long as you said no secrets, let me say what I think, O.K.?"

"Of course."

"I think this whole meeting is a blown-up charade. I don't buy it for a minute." She turned to me. "*You* want to keep your precious production together and so when I said goodbye and you thought Laurette might—"

"I wouldn't!" said Laurette. "I'm a professional."

"A professional *what*?" asked Cordy.

"Now, now," said Pam, coming between them for the thousandth time.

Lynn went on. "So you put on this elaborate show and we all kiss and make up and you go on with the game and then when Stratford's over you go ahead with the divorce."

"What divorce?" I shouted. "What're you talking about?"

She turned to Pam. "Isn't that what you told me yesterday? That you were just going to go through with this season and then file for divorce?"

I felt as though I were about to faint.

Pam blushed and said, "I was overwrought, Lynn. It's wrong of you to—and haven't we just explained the—"

"I'm not a fool, Mother. We had over an hour yesterday. Things like this . . . they don't change overnight. They *don't*."

"Of course they do," I said. "Things can change in

ten minutes."

"Not like this," she shot back. "The way she talked about you yesterday—God! She *couldn't* have changed overnight."

The discussion became more and more acrimonious and when it had reached a peak, Lynn jumped to her feet and ran off.

"Look at her," said Cordy. "Doing her ballet exit."

"She'll change her mind," said Laurette confidently.

"I don't think so," said Tim.

We all looked at him, surprised. It was the first thing he had said all afternoon.

Sixteen

Lynn did not change her mind. Pam and I went off to Canada without her, deeply disappointed. Laurette came with us. Cordelia and Tim were to follow in about two weeks.

Auditions for Lynn's replacement continued discouragingly.

Then, nine days after our arrival, a week before rehearsals were to begin, came luck. Bad luck for Lynn, good luck for us. Luck. Do we ever give it enough credit or blame? Luck. Chance. Fortune. Happenstance. Fate. Karma. My own life has been filled with luck—both good and bad—all the way.

It happened that at a ballet class, Lynn's partner slipped on the studio floor as he performed a pas de deux lift and dropped her, hurting her left ankle. She was taken at once to the Hospital for Special

Surgery at New York-Cornell.

Cordelia and Tim were informed of the accident by Marcel, the partner, and went to the hospital immediately. From there they phoned us.

"Is it serious?" I asked.

"They don't know yet," said Cordelia. "At least they haven't told us—or her."

"We'll be right down," I said.

"Yes, I think you should."

At the hospital, Dr. Richard Duncan Bunker informed us that a full series of X-rays showed that Lynn had sustained a double fracture of her left ankle.

We found her weeping, in pain and inconsolable.

When Dr. Bunker came in I asked him about procedure.

"Well," he said cheerfully, "this sort of thing isn't as serious as it once was. We'll put two or three Knowles pins in and keep her off her feet for a few days—then a crutch for a while—depends a lot on how it heals."

"No cast?" asked Pam.

"No, no," said the doctor.

"Isn't that grand, Lynnie?" said Pam. "No cast."

"Great," said Lynn, still in tears.

"And what about dancing, doctor?" I asked.

"Oh, good Lord, no," he said. "Not for some time. Walking is one thing—a natural act. But I treat dancers a good deal and I wouldn't think this one should count on getting up on point until the autumn at least. Say November."

"Oh, my God!" cried Lynn. "I'll miss the whole goddam season."

Fortunately, with her head buried in her hands, she did not see the smile that Pam and I exchanged. Good luck, bad luck.

Nevertheless, I was properly ashamed of myself almost at once. We really are a selfish species.

Pam slept at the apartment. I took a room at the hospital and we stayed with Lynn through the operation. Amazingly, within two days she was getting around on a walker.

I waited for a propitious moment to broach the subject.

No, I didn't. I *planned* a propitious moment. On her first day out of bed I had a sumptuous dinner for three sent up from Le Cirque, her favorite restaurant: pasta primavera, cold lobster mayonnaise, corn on the cob, endive and arugola salad with Lorenzo dressing, and Brie. Chocolate velvet cake and cappuccino. Martinis first, Amarone wine with the pasta, an obscenely expensive Montrachet with the lobster. And finally, daring stingers. A success in every way.

By 9:15 we were nicely oiled—I, somewhat less than the ladies because I had taken care. What wits I had left I wanted about me.

When the waiter from Le Cirque had cleared and

removed the table, Lynn produced a pack of cigarettes, removed one ceremoniously and lit it. We were astonished. She had stopped smoking three years earlier.

I was on the verge of admonishing her but held back.

Nevertheless she caught my mood. "Don't worry, Dad. It's just for this chunk of time. As long as I'm not going to be dancing, what the hell?"

"Sure," I said. "Why not?"

She laughed. "What an actor!"

"What?"

"You're seething inside."

"Not at all," I lied.

"Seething, but sweet," she said.

I leaned over and kissed her.

"Lynnie, love," I said. "I've been thinking."

"So have I," she said.

"What about?"

"About what to do with this ghastly time."

"And have you come to any conclusions?"

"Yes," she said. "I think I ought to take singing lessons. Learn to sight read and all that."

"Good idea," said Pam.

"Who knows? I may not make it to prima ballerina—in which case, there's always vulgar ol' Broadway. But did you know that when they audition dancers, they ask them to sing? And the singers dance?"

"And you know what *else* you could do?" I asked.

"What?"

CORDELIA?

"Come up to Stratford with us and play Regan."

There was a long pause. Too long, I thought. She sipped her stinger reflectively, took a last puff of her cigarette, tamped it out, finished her stinger, leaned forward and said, "Tell me the truth, Daddy. I mean the absolute no shit truth. Do you honestly think I can do it?"

"Yes," I answered. "If you want to."

"I'd hate to go on my canetta," she said. "Marcel dropping me is one thing—I can blame him. But I'd hate to drop myself." She laughed. A good sign.

I pressed on. "I wouldn't let you. If I thought you weren't going to make it, I wouldn't let you open."

"Swear?"

"Swear."

"And so do I," said Pam.

Lynn lit another cigarette and after a time said, "All right, then, let me try."

Pam went to her and they embraced.

I hurried out into the hall to call Peter. Then I went out and bought a bottle of champagne.

Seventeen

There are countless theories of acting. For instance, if an actor works himself up to *feel* anger, he may pound on a table; on the other hand, as the great French actor Coquelin insisted, "If an actor pounds on a table long enough, he will begin to *feel* anger."

I point this out to myself here because it serves to explain in some degree what happened next between Pam and me.

We moved into the lovely Findlay house and, since Lynn was still recuperating, we had her come and stay with us. Estelle for Pam, Harry for me, a local cook, and a maid completed the household.

In an intense, concentrated effort to prove to Lynn—and everyone else—that we had indeed reconciled, Pam and I overdid the outward signs of concern and care and affection. Moreover, it was necessary in the circumstances for us to share the master bedroom suite. I slept in the adjoining dressing room, and Pam fixed the king-sized bed each morning to look slept-in, with the proficiency of a great property man. And I took care of the cot in the dressing room.

Rehearsals were going well, better than any of us had expected. A few days into things I got an idea and discussed it with Pam. She liked it, so I asked Peter if he would let her play the Fool not as a man, but frankly as a woman. He objected at first but then decided to let her try it for a few days. I was right. It was a stunning revelation. Real and sensible and unique, bringing a completely new note to the part and to the entire text. It required only changing "boy" to "girl" in a few spots. Peter thought it a great improvement and the faintly lewd stuff seemed stronger coming from a female.

Pam put on her costume for an early rehearsal—colorful cap and bells and tights, which showed off her spectacular legs and a bodice which did nothing to conceal her delectable femininity.

As the Fool she lilted to me as Lear, teasingly:

> *Have more than thou showest,*
> *Speak less than thou knowest,*
> *Lend less than thou owest,*
> *Ride more than thou goest,*
> *Learn more than thou trowest,*
> *Set less than thou throwest;*
> *Leave thy drink and thy whore,*

CORDELIA?

*And keep in-a-door,
And thou shalt have more
Than two tens to a score.*

The whole company gave her an ovation and I could not help putting my arms around her—for real.

"Thank you," said Pam feelingly, then added, "you're not as dumb as you look."

It was clear that she was going to score mightily. Steal the show maybe? I would not care if she did.

The girls were all working hard, vying with one another. Which, considering the parts they were playing, was not bad.

Laurette was every bit as good as we had expected her to be.

Cordelia, apparently greatly assisted by Tim, was progressing well.

But Lynn was the great surprise. She vocalized every morning and worked on her voice. She studied the variorum with care and moved, of course, beautifully.

The long-standing tension between Cordy and Laurette was useful in performance.

Peter was helping me far beyond the call of duty, and I must say the fact that these girls really were my daughters helped me to find a Lear quickly.

More and more I believed that I had been overcome by some silly wrongheadedness about Cordelia. How could such a wild thought have entered my mind and my spirit? Did it have something to do with deepseated jealousy or insecurity or neurosis? Perhaps, I considered, when this season ends I *should* try to find some psychological help.

But for now I had neither the time nor the inclination nor the energy to pursue anything except my part. *Lear* is a ball-breaker, thought by some to be absolutely unplayable. Work absorbed me completely.

Pam was assisting me, too. On the book every night and encouraging me with a little dollop of praise now and again. Lord, what a pat on the back once in a whole does for one.

Working together, living together, the pretense of affection and amiability, gradually, insidiously began to become real. (Coquelin was right!)

And during the night following the first exciting run-through, Pam and I became man and wife again at last.

Eighteen

But, alas, our life was not destined to proceed smoothly during this production.

A call from Cordelia at 1:20 A.M.

"Can I come over and see you?" she asked, greatly agitated.

"We're asleep, love," I said. "Can't it wait until morning?"

"No it *can't!*" she said tensely.

"Come along, then."

We put on dressing gowns, went down to the kitchen and made cocoa.

Cordelia arrived in about twenty minutes, barefoot and wearing a raincoat over her nightgown. She was clearly in a highly disturbed state. No, she did *not* want any cocoa. Or any *anything*.

"What is it, darling?" asked Pam.

"I'll tell you . . . but first do you promise—both of you—to stick by me?"

"Of course."

"Certainly."

"No matter what?"

"No matter what," I said.

"All right, then. Let me tell you the whole thing and please let me finish. Don't interrupt until I'm through."

"Go ahead," said Pam.

"It's Tim. I don't know *how* I could've been so wrong about a person. He turns out to be a coldhearted chauvinistic son of a bitch. See, the trouble is maybe that we never had a crisis before—until now. Everything just went along, you know, smooth and cool and now the first time we have a problem to face he's all of a sudden a washout—I mean, a complete *blah!*"

As she stopped for breath I ignored her admonition and plunged in. "What's the problem?" I asked, fearing the worst.

"*You* know. I'm sure you can guess. And about ten seconds after I told him—five—he says, 'Well, you'll just have to get rid of it, won't you?' Just like that. No feeling, no discussion, no asking me what *I* thought or wanted to do. Just, 'Well, you'll just have to get rid of it, won't you?'"

Pam, stunned, asked, "But how could you let it

happen, Cordy?"

"Because I happened it. I wanted to."

"Without telling him?" I asked. "That wasn't fair either."

"I'm trying to *tell* you," she said tightly, "I thought he'd love it. That's how I misjudged him."

"But shouldn't something as important as that always be a mutual decision?" asked Pam. "I think so."

"I know it *now,* all right," said Cordy, in misery.

"What can we do, love?" I asked. "Tell us and we will."

"I don't know, I thought *you* might have some suggestion."

"Would you like me to talk to Tim?" I asked.

"No use, we had a real rouser, and he made it all clear."

"What clear?" asked Pam.

"He says if I think we should get married, O.K., but he doesn't want any kids. Not yet, anyway."

"Did he say why not?" I asked.

"Oh, you know, the usual. He's got to get more established, too much responsibility, tied down and all that."

"Have you tried looking at it from *his* point of view?"

"Yes. And he's wrong."

"Let me talk to him, anyway, all right?"

"Sure, if you want to. May I stay here tonight?"

"Of course."

We put her to bed.

Back in our room, Pam said, "Sweetheart, listen, let's not panic, that's the main thing. I suggest we take a pill apiece and get some sleep. We can deal with it in the morning."

"Yes," I said.

We swallowed Seconals and got back into bed.

"You're going to think me a villain," I said, "but I can't help worrying about the show. I mean, what's going to happen to it if she leaves?"

"If you want the truth," said Pam, "that's been my worry, too."

"Two villains," I said.

Whether it was the efficacy of the pills or the desire to escape the problem—we were asleep in fifteen minutes.

In the morning, I phoned Tim.

"I think we ought to talk, Tim, don't you?"

"Certainly."

"The theater?"

"Very well."

Pam and Cordelia went to the apartment to get Cordelia's things while I went over to the theater to meet Tim.

He was waiting for me when I got there. I led him into my dressing room. He sat down, looking like a criminal before the bar of justice.

"Well," I began, "this is one hell of a mess, isn't it?"

"Yes, it is. You know that I love Cordy and want to marry her?"

"She told us that."

"But I don't see why we have to rush into starting a family."

"Tim, this may come as a surprise—but I agree with you."

"You do?" he asked, brightening. "Oh, thank God!"

"But we've got a firm little spitfire to deal with. I mean, *you* have."

"*Help* me, will you?"

"I don't know, Tim. Advice. I try never to give it or to take it. It's too dangerous."

"If I could just get her to talk reasonably," he said, "but she just screams."

"Tim, listen. An old detective I used to know once said to me, 'I've been around forever, and I've learned one thing for sure. All men are pricks, and all women are crazy. No exceptions.' Now mind you, I don't think that's true, but I swear sometimes it seems so."

"I'll do my best, Alan. I'll try to reason with her again. Do you know where she is?"

"Yes," I said, "she's moving out."

"Oh, my God!"

*   *   *

It took me an hour to convince Cordelia to see him, but she finally agreed to go back to the apartment to meet with him.

She returned to us in less than an hour, in tears.

"He gets worse," she said. "He doesn't want to discuss, just to dictate. A born boss, no give-and-take, just laying down the law. I never want to see him or talk to him as long as I—"

"One more try, Cordy—"

"No."

"Cordy, listen, before you make a life decision of this kind, let's have a real meeting."

"What do you mean, a real meeting?"

"The four of us."

"Oh, no!"

"I insist, Cordy."

She looked at me. "Holy smokes! You're just like him. That's his favorite word—insist."

Nevertheless, the meeting took place that afternoon. Luckily there was no rehearsal call until 6:00.

I made them sit together on the sofa; Pam and I faced them.

"So you've had a spat—" I began.

"I wouldn't call it that," said Cordelia.

"All right, what the hell's the difference? A row, a scrap, a quarrel—a falling out. It's just as easy, by the way, to have a falling-in. Ask us. We know."

"*I'm* certainly willing," said Tim.

CORDELIA?

"Of course," said Cordelia looking at him fiercely. "On your terms."

"Wait, Cordy," said Pam.

I went on. "We've watched both of you and there was never any question in our minds but that you were two young people truly and deeply in love. If we didn't think that do you suppose we would have approved of your living together? As I see it, you've *both* been wrong. Cordy, for getting pregnant without Tim's agreement. Now, for a start will you admit that was wrong?"

"No," she said, "not wrong. But a stupid mistake, it turns out. I had no idea he's—"

"And Tim, you do agree, don't you, that just abruptly telling her what to do about it—again without discussion—was bad judgment?"

"I was in a state of shock," he said. "Sudden shock. Later on I wanted to discuss it, but it was no use."

"Why not?" asked Pam.

"She wouldn't."

"I tried," said Cordy.

Tim said, "You lost your temper and began vilifying me to a point—"

"Yes," she said, "because I suddenly saw what you really are, a mean, self-centered—"

"Cordy!"

No use. She was on her feet now standing over him. "—domineering bastard!"

"You see?" asked Tim, looking at us.

Cordelia was still in high. "Didn't we talk about having children? Didn't we many times?"

"Yes, but—"

"Didn't we even think up names we were going to call them? Girls . . . Becky and Penelope and Sarah?"

"But I didn't say—?"

"Boys . . . Ethan, Timothy, Jr. . . ." She could not go on.

I must say that Tim's cool demeanor irritated me a little, and seemed to drive her wild.

"If you want children—" he said too calmly.

"You're damn right I do!" she shouted. "But not *yours*. I wouldn't want another you in the world. You're a disgrace! I loathe you! I hope I never lay eyes on you again!"

She rushed out of the room and up the stairs. Pam followed her.

Tim and I exchanged a long look that said nothing, because there was nothing to say. He left.

I sat alone for a time, thinking, and came to the conclusion that he *was* a prick, and that she *was* crazy.

She missed the 6:00 P.M. rehearsal. We told Peter she was ill. The unprepared understudy filled in, disastrously.

The next morning Cordelia, amazingly calm and direct, announced her plans.

"I'm going to New York," she said. "I have an appointment to see Fred. I told him what it was and he said he'd get me the right man. He said I'd be able to leave New York in about a week, and I'm going straight from there to Texas, and get into Baylor and onto the track I never should have gotten off of."

I said, "You realize, don't you, that you're putting us into one tough hell of a position? Impossible, I should say."

"I do, Daddy, and if I could help it, I would, but I really have no choice. Nancy can do it."

"No, she can't. She tried last night and it was excruciating. Peter said—"

"Well *he* hired her, so why blame me?"

"Would you stay and open and then go?"

"Please don't ask me to."

"All right," I said, "I won't."

Peter sent an SOS to New York and one to London for a replacement. The problem was complicated by the fact that he was still on that resemblance kick.

In two days, Howie phoned to say he had lined up five possibles. Peter left rehearsals in charge of his capable young assistant, Hal Willy, and flew to New York.

Hal came into my dressing room before rehearsal one evening, and said, "There's a cable here for Peter from London. Do you think I should open it?"

"Of course," I said, "it's probably casting."

It was.

BELIEVE HAVE SOLVED PROBLEM STOP RADA SENIOR STELLA SMITH ABOUT NINETEEN DEAD RINGER FOR STANDISH AVAILABLE STOP PLAYED CORDELIA LAST YEAR IN RADA PRODUCTION REPORTED EXCELLENT STOP SHALL I SEND PHOTOS VIDEOTAPE OR BODY STOP JEREMY

"What do you think?" asked Hal.

"I don't know. You'd better get hold of Peter and read it to him."

Peter returned from New York the next day with astonishing news. Miss Stella Smith was on her way.

". . . tell you what I did," he said when he saw my worry. "I phoned my friend, Allan Davis, and asked him to audition the lass. He's a fine director and he gave her an A. And he says she actually *does* resemble you."

"Poor thing," I said.

"Now, now."

"I mean a *girl* to look like me?"

"Lynn does and Laurette, and they're knockouts."

"Don't mind me, Pete, I'm in a spin."

"There *is* a hitch, though."

"What?"

"Her mother won't let her come alone. So we're stuck with two fares. Economy."

"Well, what the hell? It's a pinch."

"And if she doesn't turn out, there's always a chance Cordy will change her mind or we'll just get down on our knees."

"I'm beginning to think she *has* no mind," I said.

"Tim tells me he's writing her a long letter."

"Not a chance."

Nineteen

Miss Stella Smith arrived and proved to be a major disappointment. In my opinion, she looked nothing like me—or anyone. She looked like a badly, too-heavily made-up actress. And her mother was a garrulous, Cockney, pain-in-the-ass, Mrs. Ponsonby.

"Stella," she said, gratingly, "means star, don't y'know? —and that's what she's goin' t'be. You mark my words—in my 'umble, she is already. I thought Stella Smith far better than Stella Ponsonby—for the stage, don't y'know? I know that playin' with you, sir, a lot is bound to rub off. Isn't that always the way? Ever since she was the tiniest nipper, she'd sing, she'd dance, and make an 'oly show of 'erself, and, o'course, we always gave 'er the best of trainin' too. You'll 'elp 'er, won't you, Mr. Standish? She's that frightened of you. Told me so—but it's only because she thinks so 'ighly of your actin', don't y'know?"

On and on and on.

The first rehearsal was painful. Replacements are always a sweat, trying to fit someone into someone else's shoes. The girl was nervous and terrified and gave practically nothing. She trembled a good deal and her voice was unsteady. I could see that Peter was in a state of anxiety, but he plowed bravely ahead. I wish I could say the same for myself. I simply froze and fed her the cues. The second day was a bit better. She was loosening up and beginning to relate. Now and then I saw a flash of something interesting and had a glimmer of hope, but I began to worry about that old theater disease. The fact that something is getting better gives you the illusion that it's getting good, but the fact is that it *isn't* getting good, it's just getting *better*.

On the third day, trouble. Peter had routinely asked the ladies in the company to come in without makeup. He was going to do a run-through for the makeup and hair people and wanted them to see the company in the raw, as it were.

"So no makeup at all, please, ladies." A groan from the female members of this company. "And if any of you fellows wear makeup, *you* leave it off *too*, please." A small, polite laugh.

Mrs. Ponsonby came to me. "I never 'eard of such a thing," she complained, whiningly. "Askin' a young lady to appear in public with a naked face!

CORDELIA?

Can't you stop it, sir?"

"Mrs. Ponsonby," I said harshly, "Peter Hawkins is the director of the company, and if he tells her to turn up stark naked, she'd better do it."

She was genuinely shocked. "Oh, I *say!* I never 'eard of such a thing! Starkers? I won't 'ave it! We'll leave, that we will. Leave! What sort of a place is this? Starkers, indeed!"

I burst into song. "God Almighty, Mrs. Ponsonby! Will you get away from me and leave me alone? That wasn't *serious* it was...was...a figure of speech, an example to—holy smoke, I've seen stage mothers in my time, but you take the cake!"

She drew herself up haughtily. "I'm sorry, I'm sure, if I've taken up your time. I shan't trouble you again, you may be sure, sir. Coo! I've *never* liked Americans! In the war, my mum said they used to say, 'They're overpaid, oversexed, and over 'ere!'"

I don't know what kept me from giving her a swift kick. In the *arse*.

At the rehearsals, all the girls certainly did look different, but interesting. Most of them sort of washed out and blank, others far more attractive. When Stella turned up, the company damned near froze, and when I got a good look at her, she just about stopped my clock. Talk about a spitting image! She really *did* look like me.

"It's uncanny," said Pam.

Peter got her to stand beside Laurette and Lynn. Anyone would have sworn they were sisters.

Later, Lynn said, "I owe you an apology, Dad."

"Why?"

"When I said this whole idea was a gimmick? Well, it isn't. It's great that we all sort of look alike. It gives the whole sister rivalry thing so much more tension."

There were other values in that makeup-less rehearsal that came through as we proceeded. We all became less players, and more people. By the time we got to the second act, I began to believe we had lucked out with Stella. She was a winner.

At lunch, Laurette was disturbed.

"Thanks a lot," she said ruefully.

"For what?"

"For sending for Miss Bernhardt," she said. "Lordy, she's got us outclassed, and that's a fact."

"Speak for yourself, lady," said Lynn. "She's good, but she's not *that* good."

"May I remind you both," I said, "that we're all on the same side? The better she is, the better we all look."

"Yuh, yuh," said Laurette, unconvinced.

"Dad," said Lynn, "I got to thinking during that makeup and hair run-through."

"About what?"

"About this whole Lear family resemblance idea. It certainly was fun up there the way it looked and all, but is it going to mean a damned thing when you get all full of wig and beard down to your belly button?"

"What makes you think I plan to obscure myself?"

"I don't know, I just thought."

"Peter points out that eyes, head shapes, cheekbones, noses, mouths are what convey likeness. And that's what the experts are going to concentrate on."

"Oh," she said.

When we began rehearsals I felt sorry for Stella Smith—that mother, among other things. But as time went by and she improved so dramatically, I began to admire her. By the end of the week, I had developed a warm affection for her, which in turn provided an acting problem. Cordelia is, after all, the daughter Lear turns on, and I had to make certain I was conveying the old boy's demented disaffection with her completely.

"I'm beginning to think," said Peter, "that this is going to go down in my autobiography as the Jinx Production."

"Now what?"

"Miss Smith."

"You mean Mrs. Ponsonby."

"No, Miss Smith."

"What does she want?"

"Nothing. But Canadian Equity doesn't want *her*."

I was utterly confused.

"Why not?"

"They say she's an American."

If a sandbag had fallen from the flies and hit me on the head, I couldn't have been more stunned.

Peter went on talking, but I did not hear a word. My mind was racing. *American.* And nineteen. Cordy is nineteen, almost. How could Stella be American with that mother? And, in any case, she is more British than anyone I have ever known, with the possible exception of Noel Coward. Clearly this had to be some mistake, *had* to be. Don't panic, I kept saying to myself, don't panic. You're on the edge again with this nutty obsession. Don't fall over, don't panic. Peter was still talking.

"—part of this goddam continuing international Equity feud. See, Canadian Equity is particularly pissed off about this production because what with you and Pam, the three girls and Tim, that means six American permits."

"But hell, all the rest are Canadian, aren't they?"

"Damn right. Thirty-one of them."

"So?"

"They'd prefer thirty-seven out of thirty-seven."

"It's a mix-up, I'm sure. Have you talked to them?"

"Not yet. I have them waiting."

We walked over to Stella's dressing room. She seemed jumpy, but Mrs. Ponsonby was calmly angry.

"Did you get them?" asked Peter.

"Of course, I got 'em. Why *wouldn't* I get 'em?

Silly bastards."

"Please, Mother."

"'old your tongue!"

She reached into an enormous handbag, brought forth two dark-blue British passports, and handed them to Peter. He examined them and passed them on to me. One belonged to Bridget Margaret Ponsonby, the other to Stella Smith. Stella's passport might have been a portrait by da Vinci.

"Well," I said, "this ought to do it, don't you think?"

"Without a doubt," said Peter. "Still I'd appreciate it if you could come to the hearing tomorrow morning with us."

"What 'earin'?"

"Oh, didn't I tell you? Sorry, I'm rattled. Canadian Equity Council. They insist, otherwise we can't open."

"All right."

He returned the passports to Mrs. Ponsonby, and said, "We'll pick you up at nine, all right?"

"As you wish," said Mrs. Ponsonby, insulted.

"By the way," said Peter, "I'd just as soon we kept all this confidential for the time being."

"Pam?" I asked.

"Would you mind not?" said Peter. "It's delicate."

At supper I explained to Pam as best I could. "We've got to go in to Toronto in the morning," I said. "An Equity Council meeting. Peter and I,

Stella and her mother."

"What on earth for?"

"Oh, some nonsense about her eligibility."

"But how could that be? Dues or something?"

"No, but you know, there's a lot of strain between British Equity and Canadian Equity and it's gotten down to one of those case-by-case procedures."

"Damned disgrace," she said.

"I'll be back in time for lunch."

"Did you see this letter from Cordy?"

"No. When?"

"It arrived this afternoon."

Dear Mom & Dad,

Well, it wasn't as bad as I thought. No physical pain or discomfort whatever. Dr. Anders is a superb physician. She explained every step of the procedure, so naturally that made it less scary. I feel fine and leave tomorrow for Baylor. Complicated trip. I fly from LAG American Airlines flight 85 at 9:20 A.M., arrive Dallas/Ft. Worth at 12:07 P.M., Rio Airways flight 827 at 2:45, arrive Waco, Texas, at 3:35 P.M. They say they have a student residential placement bureau that will help me find a place to live. Until that time, I'll be at the Ramada Inn, 4201 Franklin Avenue, Waco, Texas 76710 (817) 772-9440. I hope everything is going great guns and that you will invite me to come to the opening. Now, that surprised the hell out of you, didn't it? I know it surprised the hell out of *me!* Think it over.

Love,
Cordy

"She sounds fine," I said.
"Does she?"

The drive to Toronto was torture. That damned woman didn't stop talking.

"Mrs. Ponsonby," I said when it became unbearable. "Do you mind not talking for a while? I'm going over my part."

"Oh *are* you?" she said. "I'd've imagined you'd got enough of that back there, but you know best, I suppose."

"Why don't you go over *your* part as well, Stella?" She giggled. "And I'll go over *my* part, *if* you don't mind."

The atmosphere in the council room was hostile from the minute we walked in. Nine unemployed, disgruntled actors and actresses sat behind a large oak table. I thought of the Supreme Court of the United States.

The man at the center began.

"Good morning. I am Roger Crabtree, second vice-president of Canadian Equity. These ladies and gentlemen are members of the council. Our concern here today is with the question of Miss Stella Smith's contract with the Stratford Festival, a copy of which I have before me. May I ask you, Miss Smith, how long have you been a member of British Equity?"

"Three weeks," said Stella.

The council laughed.

Peter flared up. "I don't see what's so comical about that, my friends. This is Miss Smith's first professional engagement. She's just out of RADA. We *all* had to begin sometime. Even *you* people were members of Canadian Equity for three weeks at one time."

"Now, now, no need to get testy, Peter," said Crabtree. "No offense meant."

"No," said Peter. "But a good deal taken."

I spoke. "I'd like to remind the council that Miss Smith replaced one of our *American* players. My daughter, in fact."

"I must say, Mr. Standish, that *this* one could pass for your daughter."

"Yes, yes," I said, "that's the whole idea. We know all that. Can we get on with it?"

Crabtree brought his gavel down so hard that the whole council bounced, startled.

"Let *me* run this meeting, please, Mr. Standish."

"Go right ahead, but run it, don't walk it."

"Would you be good enough to let us see your passport, Miss Smith?"

Mrs. Ponsonby got it out and handed it to Stella,

CORDELIA?

who walked to the council table and gave it to Crabtree.

"Hmm," he said, examining it. "You travel quite a lot, don't you?"

"Yes, I do" she said.

"What's that got to do with anything?" asked Peter.

"Nothing, nothing, just a comment. Where were you born, Miss Smith?"

"In Birmingham, England."

"On . . . oh, yes, here it is . . . right here . . . February 26, 1962."

The date of Cordelia's birthday flashed through my mind: March 3, 1962.

"It has come to our attention, Miss Smith, that a Stella Smith was born in the United States in that same year."

I stood up and sat down. I felt lightheaded.

"So what?" said Peter. "It's a common enough name."

"Then it is your position, Miss Smith, that this person is someone other than yourself?"

"Of course!" said Mrs. Ponsonby, standing up. "This is the bloodiest silliest lot of rubbish I've ever 'eard."

"Sit down, Mrs. Ponsonby."

"I *won't* sit down!" she shouted. "And I'd like to see you make me. The girl wasn't *born* Smith, y'blasted idiots! Smith's 'er stage name. Her birth certificate doesn't say Smith."

"But how were we supposed to know *that,* Mrs.

Ponsonby?" asked Crabtree.

"Just ask!" she shouted.

"That's what we're *doing!*"

"Shall I tell you where I'm goin' directly after I leave 'ere? Find me a good barrister! The idea of draggin' my girl all the way up 'ere away from 'er work and 'er job, and these good gentlemen too, you ought to be ashamed of yourselves—"

"Now you listen to me, Mrs. Ponsonby—"

"Oh, save your breath to cool your porridge," she said, and flounced out of the room.

"Sorry, Roger," said Peter.

"Oh, never mind, it's not your fault. May we make Xeroxes of these documents?"

"Sure."

"Will you do it, Peggy?" said Crabtree, handing the passport and the contract to the secretary. She went out into another room.

Crabtree said, "We'll give you a ruling on this tomorrow."

"Why tomorrow?" asked Peter. "It looks open and shut to me."

"Yes, but we've got some new problems with British Equity, and we'll have to clear up a few points. How many Canadian Equity members are in your company again?" Peter took some papers from his pocket and consulted them. "Thirty-one."

"That includes bits, walk-ons and understudies?"

"Yes, and ASM's."

"British Equity?"

"None."

"American?"

"Well, it was six, now it's five."
"Thank you."
The secretary returned with the copies. Crabtree returned the originals to Stella.
"Is that all?" asked Peter.
"For the moment, yes. Thank you for coming."
We left.

"What did you think?" I asked Peter in the men's room before starting the drive home.
"Nothing to it," he said. "Some damned malcontent making trouble—or trying to. God! I'll bet there are a hundred Stella Smiths."
"Yes," I said. "But how many of them were born in the United States in nineteen sixty-two?"
"Thirty-three," he said.
In silence, I pondered the discrepancy in the dates: February 26. March 3.
Wonder of wonders, Mrs. Ponsonby kept absolutely quiet throughout the long drive home.

I told the whole story to Pam that night, even though Peter had asked me not to.
When I finished, she said, "Listen, do you think I could have a new gown for the *Private Lives* second act? I'm sick of the one I've got." Which gave me a rough idea as to where *her* head was.

Two days later, we received the approval of

Canadian Equity. Apparently, they were satisfied. Was I? Mrs. Ponsonby is not a person I would trust. How come they didn't ask for further documents? Birmingham birth certificate. Adoption papers. I had to check myself. The trauma was returning.

We got into *Lear* dress-rehearsal time and the usual chaos ensued. Too late nights and endless technical troubles.

Peter explained. "What makes it all so complicated is the simple production. If we had big drops and turntables and flying pieces, it would all work like a charm, but ours is actually sort of nothing—like Shakespeare's was—and to make it impressive is hard."

The reason he had taken this approach was that he had hoped we would score so decisively that someone somehow would take us to New York. I advised him not to count on it. The chances of anyone doing *King Lear* in New York, given the state of the theater, were minimal, but he is a dreamer, and I let him dream.

He worked like a demon and rode the cast hard, but my family stood up well. I was proud of them all. Laurette and Lynn, competing with Stella, made great progress and showed real promise.

After a tentative preview, we opened remarkably well.

We had invited Cordelia, but at the last moment she phoned and said she could not take the time. We

CORDELIA?

learned later that she had fallen ill. A complication as a result of the abortion, but she had lied in order to avoid upsetting us. Some kid.

Pam, as suspected, made a soaring success and basked in it happily.

The three girls also did well. The reviewers, both Canadian and American, tended to lump them together, but from my point of view, Stella outshone the other two. I hoped that I was not confusing the part with the performance. Cordelia is most certainly the best part of the three—but no, Stella was, indeed, as her monstrous mother insisted, a star.

As for myself—well, modesty forbids.

One of the troubles with repertory is that the minute you dispose of one exhausting opening, you have to begin preparing for the next. Playing *King Lear* and rehearsing *Private Lives* simultaneously was something less than a picnic, but we managed. I wanted Stella to play the maid in *Private Lives* as Cordelia had, but Canadian Equity vetoed the idea.

Twenty

It was at this point that my health began to fail. Was my head damaging my body, or was it the other way about? In these days of holistic medicine, it is difficult to know for certain. But in my case, an unholy number of factors combined and conspired to do me in.

Yes, Pam and I had gotten back together, but the fact was we both knew it would never be the same. Our life had been damaged. I had damaged it. Further, *Lear* was proving to be an even greater strain than I thought it would be. There were some nights when I thought I would not be able to get through it. Sleeping pills. More and more, stronger and stronger. Too much booze and now and then it was doubtlessly necessary for me to take a Ritalin tablet to provide sufficient artificial energy to drive me to the end.

Pam was bitterly opposed to all this stuff—she always has been—so I was forced into the degrading position of becoming a kind of closet junkie.

And then the nightmares—so appalling that I doubt I can even set them down. Waking up so drenched night after night that I had to get up and shower and change pajamas.

With all this going on, I knew that it was folly even to think of dealing with the mad imaginings that had been disturbing me for so long and that had caused such an upheaval in my life. I made a firm decision, a commitment to myself, to put the whole matter aside until the season ended. Even *I* now realized that there was a limit to what I could handle at one time.

However, two things continued to gnaw away at me. One, the suspicion or self-accusation that I was copping out, abandoning the idea because I was fearful of what the result might be. Against this I argued that I would pursue it after Stratford. Would I?

The second thing was an absolute conviction that Mrs. Ponsonby was a phony. I replayed that Canadian Equity Council meeting in my mind over and over again and I know enough about acting to recognize it when I see it—especially bad acting—and what she had delivered that morning in Toronto was the bunk. The outburst. The threat of, "I'm going to get a lawyer" (I noted she *didn't* get a lawyer) made me uneasy. What was even more ominous was her complete silence on the drive back to Stratford. It would take something extraordinary to shut that woman up. What was it?

But I knew that it was essential for me to put those two worries aside if I was to get through the season with my sanity intact—if, indeed, I had not already parted with it.

Stella came into my dressing room one evening just before the *Private Lives* half-hour call and asked if she could understudy Louise, the maid. The current understudy was leaving for an industrial film job in Detroit.

"You'll have to ask Peter," I said.

"I already have, and he says it's all right with him if it's all right with you."

"And what about Canadian Equity?" I asked.

"That's all right too," she said. "Because Tilda quit."

"Fine, then."

"Oh, thank you!" she said passionately. *"Thank you!"* She rushed out as though to announce to the world that she had just been signed to play Scarlett O'Hara in the original production of *Gone with the Wind*.

I reflected that here was one stage-struck little lady.

*   *   *

Not long afterward I happened to drop into the theater while an understudy rehearsal was in progress. Stella was playing Louise so brilliantly that I thought for a moment she was someone else.

Now that she was in the *Private Lives* company, she took to coming to the theater for every performance, not only on *Lear* nights. She would watch *Private Lives* straight through each time, sometimes from the front and often from the wings. She was clearly one of those who was completely and thoroughly absorbed in the theater.

As a rule, Pam hates anyone watching from the wings, but she said nothing about Stella.

I asked her. "Do you mind the girl in the wings? I can tell her not to."

"Oh, no, she's all right. She reminds me of myself at her age, hungry and avid to learn."

"She's a nice kid."

"*And* a sexpot," said Pam. "Again like me at nineteen. She's got half the boys in the company smitten. I expect dueling to break out at any moment."

It had not occurred to me, but now that Pam had mentioned it, I realized that it was true. The lads were constantly swarming around her, bringing her food and drink and even flowers. Tim, by the way, was among them.

Considering it all objectively, she was indeed a stunner. Large, limpid eyes; sensuous, generous lips; matchless figure and legs; and, instead of breasts, an authentic classical *poitrine*.

Why then, I wondered, did *I* not respond or react to her in any way? Probably, I thought, because I was too bloody fatigued to react or respond to anyone or anything. Four *Lears* a week, and four *Private Lives* had taken a toll. Or was I reaching—had I reached—that time of life? I didn't want to believe it. In any case, not so. There was a tall, sloe-eyed, athletic type in the company—Diana—who was Pam's standby. And once I had seen her windsurfing in her bikini at the lake I could hardly keep my hands off her.

Pam fell violently ill one night and woke me at about four in the morning.

"I think we'd better send for the doctor," she whispered.

I called him without delay.

"He's on the way," I said, "I'll get Estelle and Harry."

"No," she said, "not Harry, just Estelle."

I called Estelle on the intercom, then asked, "What is it, love?"

"I'm hemorrhaging," she said.

"Oh, Jesus!"

Estelle came in and together we did what little we could until the doctor arrived. Pam's menstrual cycle had always given her great difficulty and was a constant source of worry to us both. We'd consulted doctors everywhere. Some methods helped with temporary relief, but basically the problem remained. I had researched the question endlessly, and had come up with a number of remedies that seemed for a time to be more or less efficacious. Cramp Bark Tea, for example, but its use required careful attention to the dates, and in the pressure-cooker of this season, Pam had neglected to give the matter sufficient attention.

Dr. Jacobi provided a powerful pain killer at once, then proceeded to deal with the condition and its symptoms.

By 6:00 A.M., Pam was resting quietly. The doctor and I went down to the kitchen where Estelle got us an early breakfast.

"What about the matinée today?" I asked.

"—depends on her," he said. "She'll know. If she feels up to it, well and good, I have no objection . . . what a treat, *American* bacon!"

By noon Pam was awake and chipper and whistling.

"Quite a man, that Jacobi," she said, "I'd like to adopt him."

"Listen," I said, "are you sure about the matinée?"

"Sure, sure—you trying to get rid of me?"

"Hardly," I said. "You know how I love playing *Private Lives* with you. All that nuzzling and cuddling and kissing."

"I know," she said. "It's about the only chance we get these days and nights. Loving in public—for a living. I'll be all right, I promise you."

We had a light lunch and drove over to the theater, instead of walking as we usually did.

Just after half-hour had been called, an over-excited Estelle came rushing into my dressing room.

"Come quick, Alan! Oh, my God! Come quick."

I stopped only long enough to slip on a pair of shorts and ran over to Pam's room. She was lying on the floor, more pale than I had ever seen her.

Estelle and I got her onto the couch.

"Get Dr. Jacobi again!" I yelled, "right away."

Estelle ran.

I broke an ammonia capsule under Pam's nose. Her head twitched, and she moaned.

"I'm all right," she said. "Perfectly all right." Then she fainted again.

Cold compresses, legs up, calling her name.

Hal came in. I saw Stella's concerned face in the doorway behind him.

"Can *I* do anything?" he inquired.

"Not right now, thanks. The doctor's on his way, but what you *can* do is get Diana ready to go on." (Guilty thoughts of playing it with her. Exciting.) "I'm sorry I can't let her have this room, but Estelle'll work it out from somewhere."

He looked stricken.

"What's the matter?" I asked.

"Diana," he mumbled. "Now don't get sore, Alan."

"Now what?"

"Diana," he said, unsteadily. "She's a standby, you know, not an understudy."

"What about it?"

"Well, that means she doesn't have to report to the theater, she just has to call in at half-hour."

"And?"

"And she did, and I told her Pam was in. So she's gone off."

"Gone off where?"

"Search me."

"Well, find her, you half-wit!"

"Wait a second, Alan, I don't have to take that kind of abuse from you. Goddam it! *I* was the one said we should have the standbys stand by in case of something happening during the performance, and *you* said you would never make a replacement during the middle of a show. *You* said."

"And I wouldn't."

"Well, that's why Diana's not here. So get off my back."

"And what do you propose to do?"

"I don't know. Cancel, I suppose."

"I'm all *right,*" said Pam with a dry tongue. "I'm *perfectly all right.*" She got up from the couch and staggered to her dressing table. "No, I'm not," she said, and put her head down on the shelf.

"Relax, love. Jacobi'll be here any minute."

"Would you let *me* do it?" said a voice. I looked up into the mirror. Standing behind me was Stella. I turned, faced her and regarded her with amazement. At that moment, she looked all of fourteen. Despite the crisis, I laughed. I couldn't help it. She was so brave, so show business that I could not help putting my arms around her.

"You're a terrific child, Stella," I said, "but—"

"I swear to God I know the part. I'm word perfect, and I know the staging."

"I'm sure you do, love, but without a single rehearsal . . . I honestly couldn't take the chance. You'd be fine, I'm sure, but *I'd* go to pieces."

"Please?" she begged.

"Stella, it would look too preposterous. I'm forty-eight. Elyot is supposed to be thirty-eight. Pamela's forty-three. Amanda is supposed to be about thirty. You're *nineteen* for God's sake."

"I'm an actress."

I will not attempt to describe the way she spoke those words. It was almost as though she had said, "I'm a goddess" or "I'm an angel" or "I'm Superwoman." She had me.

And, caution to the winds, I said, "All right, then. Tell Estelle to get the wardrobe out of here and help you."

She did not wait to do so—but rushed into the room and began gathering up the frocks and shoes and jewelry and props for Act One.

"And if they don't fit," I called after her, "wear *anything.*"

"They'll *fit,*" she called back, and was off.

Dr. Jacobi arrived and took Pam home. Estelle sent for Lynn and Laurette to meet them there. We held the curtain no more than five minutes. I needed those five minutes to pull myself together and collect my thoughts.

Hal went out and made the announcement to the customary sounds of dismay, but there were no refunds.

The opening balcony scene. I am alone finally, my back to the adjoining balcony separated from mine by a small hedge. I sense the audience stir in anticipation as Amanda comes on. I hear the champagne glasses tinkle on the tray. Is she nervous? Too nervous? The music cue. "Someday I'll Find You." I begin to sing, softly. I sound especially good to myself. Am I trying to impress her? Encourage her? What?

Presently, as indicated, she joins me in song. I do my reaction, jump up, twirl about and look across the hedge. She is sitting there singing, pretending not to know that I am where I am. She finishes the song, stands to face me. She speaks her first line:

"'Thoughtful of them to play that, wasn't it?'"

My line is:

'What are you doing here?' But I can hardly get it

CORDELIA?

out, because I cannot for a moment believe what I see and hear before me. Not Stella, nineteen—but Amanda, thirty. Her hair, her worldly air, her stance, her expression—the way she is holding her drink. Amanda. "I'm an actress," she had said, and now she was proving it.

Eventually, I managed to pick up my cue and we continued to play the scene. The act moved briskly and I was aware that this was perhaps the single most astonishing theater adventure I had ever been part of.

I avoided her at both intermissions, not wanting to break the spell.

At the end, a solid reception. I felt constrained to make my first curtain speech of the year.

"Thank you, ladies and gentlemen. I don't know how many of you are aware that you saw some theater history made here this afternoon. My wife was taken ill quite suddenly directly before the performance. She's all right now. (Applause.) Her standby was unaccountably not available, and so this remarkable young actress volunteered to keep the curtain up—and I do not need to tell you how beautifully and brilliantly she did so." (Prolonged applause.) I moved back, took Stella's hand, brought her front and center. "I offer her my thanks and Pamela's and the company's and the Festival's, and I predict for her an infinite future." (Standing ovation.)

Stella bowed, charmingly and gracefully. No

playacting, no girlish tears, no amateur giddiness, no Miss America nonsense. She was professional. She had done her job, and that was that.

I went home immediately. Pam and the girls were there, having tea.

I reported in some detail what had happened at the theater. They were not surprised.

Pam said, "In that case, you won't mind terribly if I stay off tonight?"

"I think it would be only sensible," I said.

"I'm all right," she said. "It's only that I don't seem to have my *knees.*"

As a general theatrical rule, understudies give a credible or adequate performance when they are called upon to go on, but then get worse and worse if they have to continue to play.

Not the case with Stella, whose performance that night was even better than the matinee had been. She was more relaxed and confident, and more skillful in handling the audience and its reactions.

But I noticed something interesting. Interesting to me, at any rate. Despite the erotic physical display and excitement in the Elyot-Amanda scenes, the passionate kisses, the sexual embraces, I felt nothing as a man, only as an actor.

Has anyone ever been able to explain the hidden

mystery of sexual attraction, or its absence? A life in the theater and films and television has brought me in close contact with some of the most attractive and libidinous creatures of my time. A few have been, I am certain, the objects of the private fantasies of millions of men. Illustrious pin-ups.

I have tasted my share of forbidden fruit, but it has often surprised me to find that my physical response was seldom to the standard desired model. On a few occasions, it was made eminently clear to me that it was there for the taking—usually on lonely locations, or on boring tours—but I seldom availed myself of these offers. I can't explain my own reactions which are whimsical and often unorthodox.

That theater maid Pam accuses me of having: True. One long look exchanged with her and I knew I could not rest until our relationship had been consummated. She was Welsh, small, rather dumpy, short-haired and spectacled, but her sexual magnetism was powerful beyond resistance. I was not disappointed.

"I like a lot of kissing," she said on our first encounter. And when we began, I could see why. She had developed kissing into a high art, and half an hour of it was not unusual.

For the rest, she and everything about her—body, clothing, habitation—was pristine and fragrant. She was a bed of roses, and when she went off with the soundman to get married, I was bereft. Until one night in the lobby of the Metropolitan Opera House during an intermission, when I encountered the handsome, white-haired dream of loveliness who had taught makeup at the American Academy of Dramatic Arts when I was a student there. She had retired, was then seventy-odd, trim and sleek and saucier than ever. I was alone (Pam *hates* opera); she was alone (a habitual practice). Her invitation to come up to her nearby apartment for a drink after the performance was quickly accepted and ended with a cloudburst in her bedroom.

So who can explain it? And it works the other way about, as well. There have been some—many—on whom I had designs and who I thought would be easy, simply a matter of making the move. I am still surprised at my list of failures. I was simply not attractive to them.

I know we are all square or round pegs or square or round holes. (That came out more grossly than I had intended, but it is what I believe.)

Pam returned for *Lear* the following night and resumed her schedule with *Private Lives*. She sent Stella $50 worth of long-stemmed roses with a note of thanks for filling in so brilliantly. Stella was genuinely overcome.

We were having tea together at her place. It was

Pam's afternoon at the hairdresser's. Mrs. Ponsonby was in Toronto on some business of her own.

"When did you first know you wanted to be an actress?" I asked.

"I don't know," she answered. "I can't remember when I *didn't* want to be."

"But the idea must have been stimulated *somehow*. Did you see a play, or a movie, or read a book? The telly, as you call it?"

"I'm not quite sure," she said. "It may have begun with all that dressing up I used to do. I was always dressing up and pretending to be someone else. A hated aunt, or a loved one. Or was it the dancing, I wonder? I'm told that I began dancing at the age of two, or even less."

"My daughter Lynn is a beautiful dancer."

"I know . . . It was always a cry for attention I expect, for applause, or approval."

"What was the first play you ever saw—do you remember? Or film?"

"Don't be daft," she said, laughing. "Do I remember? How could I *forget?* Film first. It was *Mary Poppins*. They showed it at school, at the Christmas season one year. I was in the first form. Each of the forms was shown it once. There were nine, so I saw it nine times. I still can't explain how I managed that caper, but I did. Ran away from my own form, and sneaked in, no doubt."

"—reminds me a bit of *my* early theatergoing days. No dough. So I'd acquire a program, usually one that had been thrown away in the street—our playbills are uniform, you know, not like yours. And I'd go around to a theater—any theater—and mingle with the people on the sidewalk in the first intermission, then drift in with them, find an empty seat and see the rest of the play."

"Super!"

"Peter says it's that training that makes me disrespect all first acts. He says I never get going until the second."

"He's wrong," she said seriously.

I laughed. "I remember going to the Forty-sixth Street Theater one night to do my thing. There I was, program in hand, waiting for the first intermission. I waited a good long time because no one had told me that that was a show played *without* intermission."

"Oh, no!" she said, dismayed.

For a moment, I thought she was going to cry.

"And what about theater?" I asked.

"*Peter Pan,* of course. I was six, and I haven't got over it yet."

"What will you do," I asked, "when we finish here?"

She shrugged. "Go home, I suspect, and look for a job."

"Have you considered giving California a try?"

"Heavens, no!"

"Why not?"

"Terrified. And at any rate, I want to stay in the theater for a time—until I'm somebody and get a

CORDELIA?

proper film offer."

"You're somebody now, Stella."

Her face took on a serious expression. "Well, if I am, Alan, you had a great deal to do with it. You and Pam. I love you both."

"And we love you. You've proved to be one of the dearest surprises of our life."

"Thank you."

"You can imagine what a blow it was to us when our daughter Cordelia suddenly decided to defect."

"And I can't tell you how glad I am she *did!*"

"Well, in the circumstances, I suppose it's all for the best. She's happier, and so are you—and confidentially, so am I."

"Truly?"

"Truly."

"Now, may I ask, what's all this with you and Tim?"

"Lordy Lord," she said, "I might've known. The gossipiness of any theatrical company in the world."

"None of my business, of course, but—"

"Yes, it is. Tim's asked me out a few times and I've gone. He's all right. Good actor. I know about him and Cordelia."

"How?"

"He told me."

"How much?"

"Why, that they were in love and that she left him."

"Did he tell you why?"

"No."

"Good. And now what?"

"I told him I felt dicey about it all, as though I were a standby who'd gotten on, the way I did in *Private Lives* the other day. I'm certainly not involved with him or going to be. At any rate I get the feeling he hasn't given up on Cordelia. He says he's going to Texas when he finishes here."

"News to me. Stella, this next is sort of confidential, but I'd like you to know because of plans and schedules."

"Yes."

"There's some talk—vague, to be sure, and nothing's settled yet, not by a long shot—"

"Oh, Lord, what is it?" she asked. "I'm on tenterhooks."

"Well, it's about the possibility of this whole thing going to Broadway."

She was on her feet in an instant. "Oh, blimey!"

"Roger Stevens is coming up next week or the week after. If it all works out it'll be a few weeks in Washington, and then New York."

"I'm going to faint," she said.

"It'll mean virtually a whole new company, I'm afraid, except for Pam and me, Tim and the girls. *You're* going to be a problem. American Equity. They're tough."

"I know."

"Trouble is, you're not a star, you see."

"My mother thinks I am," she said.

"Yes, and so do I. But let's wait and see. I wanted

to tell you so that you didn't make any definite plans until ours are."

In her confident exuberance, she came to me and hugged me tightly.

"I love you," she said.

"Ditto," I said. "And thank you for the best tea I've had since I played in *The Importance of Being Earnest.*"

Twenty-One

The Kennedy Center people did come up the following week to see our production of *King Lear*.

The company was alerted and rose to the occasion. It was by far the best performance we had ever given.

Afterward, a supper conference at the Inn.

Our guests began by saying flattering things to Pam and to me and to Peter. We basked in the praise. Then one of them said, "I don't think there's a quarter in it."

We were instantly deflated.

"Why not?" asked Peter.

"Because, there never *has* been in *Lear*."

"Oh."

"That doesn't mean that we shouldn't try to do it."

Life returned to my body.

"It'll have to be underwritten, of course. We'll try to get some of the business/art boys up to have a look at you. How long have we got?"

"Three and a half weeks," said Peter.

"Short notice, but let us try."

"We'll play for scale," I said. "All of us."

"Yes," said a Kennedy man, "you'll have to."

Each night thereafter there were rumors about who was out front. IBM, Ford Motor, Honeywell.

The Kennedy people turned up again the night before we closed, saw the performance, and came back afterward to announce it was all set.

I let out a whoop. I couldn't help it. Pam was ecstatic, especially when they told us that we would play *Lear* and *Private Lives* in repertory.

"No one," said the managing director, "can play *Lear* eight times a week. Anyway, we'll do fine. *Private Lives*'ll help support the big one."

The champagne flowed.

The Kennedy Center people and Peter and I made a strong and special appeal to Equity to allow us to bring the Stratford company down. Not a chance.

"I didn't think they would," I said.

"Well, it was worth a bash," said Peter.

"I sure hope all this ends someday," I said irritably. "We don't keep out foreign musicians or painters, or dancers or writers or athletes—

why actors?"

"Give up," said Peter. "Give it up."

"When can we go?" asked the Kennedy production supervisor.

"Three weeks?" asked Peter in reply. "If God is good, I might find a cast in that time."

"Could you make it two?"

"I could say yes, but with no confidence."

"Very well, then. Three it is."

The date books came out and the calendars and arrangements began. I had never been more excited. It was going to be the top of my life, I knew it, the apex of my career. After all, how many American actors get to play *Lear* in New York?

Another family conference. I presided in a way that made Lynn twit me.

"Look at him!" she said, laughing. "He's *still* playing Lear."

"Damn right!" I said. "And if you don't behave yourself, I'll cut you off without a shilling or a piece of the country."

"Not me," she shot back. "You can't. That's not in the script. I'm Regan, remember. Cordelia's the one you cut off."

"Tim's gone out to see her," said Laurette. "Did you know that?"

"Why, no," Pam said. "Are you sure?"

"Absolutely."

I asked, "Does she know he's coming?"

"No idea."

"What do you think will happen?" asked Pam.

"Anybody got a guess?"

"They'll make it," said Lynn.

"No way," said Laurette.

I reflected that if Lynn had said no, Laurette would have said yes. I know my daughters.

"Want to bet?" challenged Lynn.

"It makes no sense," said Laurette. "Unless people start having dogs and cows and horses in Shubert Alley. What kind of a life could that possibly be? Or marriage? Him an actor and her a vet."

"He," I corrected, "and she."

"Daddy, will you *stop*? I'm twenty-two years old and I speak fluent English. Like a native almost."

"What you *don't* know is," said Lynn, "that she's ready to chuck it and would in a minute to get him back."

"Ridiculous," said Laurette.

"I don't know," said Pam. "She did it before for him—she might again. And wouldn't that solve a lot of problems for you, love?"

"How?" I asked.

"By having her back in the company. Equity's never going to let you use Stella."

"Yes," I said, preoccupied. "Yes."

Why didn't I say what I thought? What I thought was that I preferred Stella by far in the part. Cordy was all right, but no more. And Broadway is the toughest street in the world, with the highest standards. To hell with nepotism and Peter's gimmick. I hoped that Cordy and Tim would not get together, not if it meant her returning to the company. I was a little ashamed of myself. Not much, though.

"Now then, ladies," I said. "Give me your undivided, please." Surprisingly, they did. "As I have reminded you before, my old friend Ben Franklin once said: 'Don't waste time'"—they all three joined me and in unison finished the adage—"'because that's the stuff life's made of.'"

"Correct," I said. "Now. We have three weeks to deal with, and the question is how best to employ them."

"I'm going to stay in bed," said Laurette.

"Who with?" asked Lynn.

"With whom?" I said absently.

"Lynn!" said Pam, shocked.

"Paris," said Lynn. "A week in Paris and a week in London. That's me."

"Key West for me," said Laurette. "If I can get someone to go with."

"I've got to stay here, you know," I said, "and work with Peter—but please, Pam, don't feel *you* have to."

"Thank you," she said. "That's very thoughtful."

"Why don't you come with me?" asked Lynn. "Please, it'll be great."

"I was thinking the same thing," said Pam. She came to me. "You really wouldn't mind?"

"Of course I'll mind. I wish I could go with you but you can use the break."

"You know what you are?" asked Pam.

"What?"

"A nice man."

So it was arranged.

Laurette found not one but three friends, and two happy couples flew off to Key West.

Pam and Lynn, after four days of whirlwind shopping and preparation, were on their way to France.

The fact is that Peter could easily have done what needed to be done without me, but I wanted time to myself to try to solve my problem. Peter cooperated and made a great point with Pam about needing me in New York.

The day after I saw Pam and Lynn off on Pan Am I went to work.

I began with the Yellow Pages, which Frank Loesser once referred to as the "greatest book in the world."

"Give me the Yellow Pages," he said, "and I can build the Empire State Building, open and operate a Hungarian restaurant or produce a show."

I went through the listings for private investigators, picked out a few that sounded good, and began phoning. One of them assured me that they had not merely a liaison in England, but a full-fledged, legitimate branch. That sounded like the one for me, and I made an appointment to meet with the chief supervisor at his office. He turned out to be British—Archie Markham—and so like a stage Scotland Yard type that I almost laughed.

CORDELIA?

"Now, how can we be of assistance, Mr. Standish?" he asked.

"I want to find out all I can as quickly as I can, about a Mrs. Bridget Margaret Ponsonby of Birmingham, England, who is temporarily in the United States."

"And how much do you know about her at the present time?"

"Not much. Here are a few photographs."

I handed him some Stratford Polaroids and snapshots.

"Good," he said. "This is most helpful."

"And this." I gave him a Xerox of her passport.

"Excellent. Any other information? Her present address?"

"Yes. The Hotel Wellington, Seventh Avenue and Fifty-fifth Street."

"Good."

"She's there with her daughter."

"Name?"

"Stella Smith."

"Age?"

"Nineteen."

"Occupation?"

"Actress."

"Employed?"

"Not at the moment, but may be soon. By the way, I don't know how long the Wellington address will be good, but I'll let you know if it changes."

"And what, may I ask, is Mrs. Ponsonby's occupation?"

"I don't know. Professional nuisance, I guess."

He missed the joke, if it was a joke.

"Do you know . . . do you have her Birmingham address?"

"Yes." I had gotten it from the Festival office and gave it to Markham.

"Husband's name?"

"I don't know."

"Occupation?"

"I don't know."

"Right you are. Oh, come in Rusty, come in."

A tall, redheaded bruiser made his way into the office.

"This is Mr. Alan Standish, Rusty. Rusty Schneider."

We shook hands.

"Rusty will be your New York-based investigator. He'll be following through on the case and keep you informed of our progress. You can call him at any time for a status report, or to give him any new information that might come to your attention."

"You do understand, Mr. Schneider," I said, "that there's some urgency as to time?"

"There usually is," he said, and exchanged a knowing smile with Markham.

We exchanged cards, shook hands all around and parted.

I felt silly and strong at the same time.

The Yellow Pages again. "Psychiatrists." I know,

CORDELIA?

it's peculiar to pick a shrink in the Yellow Pages, but they *are* listed and they *are* legitimate. I didn't want to ask friends for a recommendation . . . the whole subject was too personal, too upsetting. I decided to go all out, pick a female with an interesting name. Dr. Shanti Ray Rau. Exotic.

I phoned and made an appointment. I hoped I would be able to handle her English. Communication is tough enough in a matter such as this.

I need not have been concerned. Her English was better than mine.

She was tall, dark, and—no, not handsome as well, but piercing eyes, a large nose, beautiful lips, a soothing manner. The only disappointment was that she was wearing a trim Chanel suit; I had hoped for a sari.

"It is a pleasure to meet you, Mr. Standish. I have seen you on the stage."

"Oh, good. I feel less of a stranger then."

"I admire you greatly. I love the theater. It is one of the principal reasons why I practice in New York. There are other places where life would be perhaps simpler and the work more lucrative, but I must be in New York. My husband and I, we are both, as you say, theater buffs. Yes, often a play we enjoy we go to see again and again."

"Buffs, indeed," I said.

"Speaking of stranger, of feeling less one, let me tell you one of my policies. Please call me Shanti and allow me to address you as Alan."

"By all means."

"It will be easier. You are—no, *we* are—on the verge of intimate exchange, as you can imagine."

"Yes."

"I notice, Alan, that there is no referral information on your registration."

"No."

"How, then, did you come to me?"

"The Yellow Pages," I said.

"The Yellow Pages!" she repeated with some astonishment. "Extraordinary." She laughed. "I must say this is the first time such a thing has happened. Most people ask their doctors to recommend someone."

"Yes. Well, I have several fine doctors in my life who are also friends, but this matter is too private to discuss even with them. And if I asked them to recommend a head doctor, they'd be suspicious. No, this is a personal—a deeply personal—problem."

"Begin, please," she said.

I took a deep breath and plunged in. "Shanti, I am suffering from a delusion that may not be a delusion. An obsession? It's driving me insane, if it hasn't already done so. Neurotic? Paranoid? Yes, I know I'm using a lot of lingo that I don't understand. But I'm trying to get it all out." I paused, but she said nothing. Why not? I was irritated, then presumed that it was part of her technique. "I have three daughters," I went on. "Twenty-three, twenty-two, nineteen. I love my wife. We've been married almost twenty-four years. In that time, I've had a few affairs—casual adventures, nothing ever serious or lengthy or threatening. She usually knows about them. Not always, *sometimes*. I think she's had a few, too. Not as many as I have, but a few—that I know about, that is. All right. It's important for you to know that. Wait. I'm not doing this right, am I? I said delusions—or did I say obsession?—well, whatever. I suppose I'd better tell you what it is, and then start from the beginning again. May I have a glass of water, please? . . . Thank you. My delusion, obsession, is that one of my daughters—the youngest one, Cordelia—she's nineteen. Well, my obsession is that she's not my daughter, that I'm not her father." Still silence. "I can't say when the suspicions first began. It must've been so slight, so subtle that I wasn't even aware of it. The other two look like me, a lot like me. She doesn't. She looks more like her mother. For years everyone thought and said how much she did look like me, and I thought so too. But later on I began to realize that it was what people said to a doting father, and what a doting father wanted to believe, regardless of reality. Then puberty and those two tiny protuberances on her chest turned into little breasts, and she began to wear a bra, and from that moment on she really became more and more like her mother."

I had been looking down. Now I looked up. She was smiling at me, beatifically, but still said nothing. A shadow of a gesture bade me continue. "Well, so much for that—for the resemblance factor. There are other things, too. The other two daughters have always been theatrical to some degree. Not this one, not Cordelia. Now that I think of it, she never even liked *going* to the theater—or even to the movies. And when she did go with us, she'd be bored or restless and squirmy. She'd read the program from cover to cover while the play was on. Once I caught her reading a book she'd brought with her, and I raised hell. She didn't like to play games like charades with the family, either. Caused all sorts of ruckuses. Then somewhere along the line—animals. I swear I think she began to like animals more than people. I'm sure she does now. She's at school, at college in Texas, studying to be a vetenarian. A veterinarian. Now, I don't know a hell of a lot about the whole complicated question of heredity versus environment. I've only read one book on the subject of inherited characteristics, and I know that there are many actors and actresses whose children *haven't* gone into the theater, so when I can put my brain onto the matter and be sensible and rational, all is well. But then, something stranger and deeper takes over. Instinct, belief—shall I try to see how many words I know that describe how I feel? I mean *why* I feel what I feel? Instinct, belief. I know, I've already said those, but assuredness, certainty, certitude. Is there a difference? Positive, assured. Well, you get the idea. And then my reason is overwhelmed and obliterated and I simply know what I know in my bones, in my blood. . . . A few months ago, I made the bad mistake of hinting at it in a way I thought was subtle, and I came close to ruining my marriage and my life and my career. And all because

CORDELIA?

of something that, when I look at it objectively, convinces me that I must be cockeyed. I did *King Lear* this summer in Canada. We're doing it in New York this season. My three daughters played my three daughters in the play—that is, until my daughter, Cordelia, I mean the *real* Cordelia, just quit. So we had to replace her. The director wanted someone who looked like me, and he conducted a big search and found a girl in London who really does, and I keep studying her and trying to figure out how she could possibly be my daughter. She couldn't, of course, but there's a sample of my madness. She was born in England. I wasn't anywhere near England even remotely around the time that would make such an eventuality possible. Peter—he's the director—found a look-alike because, as I say, he searched. In time I'm sure he could have found dozens. There. Doesn't that prove I'm batty? I swear to Christ, listening to myself tell it I sound crazy to myself. There's one more thing—which may or may not be important—but I don't think I can tell it to you now or today. I'm tired, this is tiring. I didn't know it was going to be. May I stop?"

"It is entirely up to you, Alan."

"Thank you. Don't you ever say anything?"

She laughed lightly. "When it is my turn, yes."

"I'll see you tomorrow, then?"

"I look forward to it. A suggestion. Please do not plan too much in advance what you are going to say or how you are going to say it. In other words, no rehearsing, please."

"I understand."

She offered her hand; a warm, strong, enveloping grip.

> Hotel Raphael
> 17, Ave. Kleber
> Paris XVI

Dearest,

This was the all-time Olympic-championship best idea ever! Troubles seem at least 3,000 miles away and in another language. We have walked and walked. I said to Lynnie this afternoon, "Why is it that we always see so much more when we're abroad?" "Because we look," she said. I thought at first she was a smartass. Now I see that she is smart.

Do you think you could get Phil Bosco for Edmund? He would be divine.

Call Cordy please.

To the Comédie tonight to see their new production of *Cyrano,* so please forgive me while I go back and continue to look over the text.

You know how much I love you.

> Pam

CORDELIA?

A postcard from Key West:

Dear Dad,

It's better than I thought it was going to be. You'll be pleased to know that I haven't thought of *King Lear* once! Nor do I intend to. I am black and blue from windsurfing—my new passion. Otherwise in elegant, excellent order. Miss you. Love you.

Regan

Hotel Raphael
17, Ave. Kleber
Paris XVI

Dear Nose-to-the Grindstone,

Havingwonderfultimewishyouwerehere. (I considered ending this letter right here but then considered that if it should happen to reach you in one of your famous "moods" I would probably be out of a job. So I press on.)

We saw a *breathtaking Cyrano* at the Comédie Française the other night and what impressed me almost as much as the play and the production was the audience. Lots of children, all dressed up and the little girls in white gloves. Theatergoing a great event here. I was very moved.

But thinking back on it and not trying to butter you up, I swear—I thought our *Lear* stood up to the Comédie standard just fine. So there.

I am having, thanks to you, one *whale* of a time. So thanks to you.

Your loving daughter,
Lynn Annabella Standish

I was impressed. Three communications from the family in three days. Nothing from Texas. Did it mean anything? Something to mention to Shanti? I'll see.

And somewhere about this time the dreams began—as if I didn't have enough to devil me.

Dreams have never much interested me. Once, when I played a psychiatrist in a Hal Ashby movie, I did some research on the subject and consulted the illustrious Dr. Benton at USC.

"Dreams are meaningless," he said. "The floating garbage of the mind. And in spite of the wild claims of certain men in the field, I don't believe there is anything to be learned from them or their analysis. To my mind, there's not much difference between Freudian dream analysis and the mumbo jumbo dream books that used to flourish up in Harlem."

But then of course he was anti-Freud.

During my time in the army, I awoke in the

barracks in the middle of the night and saw my buddy, Craig, sitting on his cot beside mine, fully dressed. Just sitting.

"What's the matter?" I whispered.

"—can't sleep," he said. "It's my dreams. They bore me."

Well, I don't recall that mine ever bored me—they were usually tied into my work or rehearsals or performances—but they certainly didn't interest me until this upsetting series. These were intensely personal.

The first one I recall was this: Our bed, but expanded enormously. We are all in it—Pam, Lynn, Laurette, Cordelia and I. Breakfast. I reach for Cordy. As I do so, her pajamas disappear, as do mine. Now she is under me and has skillfully adapted the positioning of her legs and thighs to assist my entry. We are in free-floating action. Pam and the girls continue their breakfast, glancing over at us from time to time. Pam butters a croissant and hands it to Cordy who begins to eat it ravenously. When I object, she slaps me. I get away from her and protest to Pam. *She* slaps me, then joins Laurette and Lynn in wild laughter.

I wonder if I should tell it to Shanti. I don't want to.

A call from Rusty Schneider.

"I don't know if this will interest you or not, but I've got a few snippets already from Birmingham."

"Anything," I said.

"Well, her name—maiden name—is Tobbit. T-o-"

"Never mind. I *know* how to spell it."

"All right. She was born in London—not Birmingham—November twenty-one, nineteen thirty-nine. Married a Sam Ponsonby, Birmingham police officer (nickname Smasher) July seventeen, nineteen seventy-one. Her first marriage. She and Ponsonby were divorced in nineteen seventy-seven and she moved to London and took a job as barmaid at the Golden Crown in Kings Road. Any of this any good to you?"

"Yes," I said. "Fine. When will you have more?"

"Every day, I wouldn't be surprised."

"Thanks."

"You got it."

I looked forward to seeing Shanti. Simply talking it out was proving to be a valuable catharsis. Unburdening myself. Ben once pointed out that all expulsion is pleasant or brings relief: pissing, nose-blowing, vomiting, belching and so on. Maybe emptying the mind of its excrement works in the same way? The expulsion of needless, useless, self-perpetuating poisons. In any case, thinking aloud has helped to clarify much.

"I have an investigative agency getting me as

CORDELIA?

much information as possible about Mrs. Ponsonby and Stella. Christ! Another form of paranoia, isn't it?" Shanti said nothing. Did that mean she agreed or was it simply a continuation of her methodology? "Everything's beginning to shape up legitimately. I mean piece by piece. When and where Stella was born and so on. I hear from my wife and the two older girls quite often, surprisingly often. But not a word from Cordy. Well, I suppose it's getting settled in a new place, new life—maybe purposely cutting the family ties? Do I seem to be asking a lot of questions? Too many?" Silence, of course. "I have a matchless friend, a scientist, in Cincinnati, who says that questions are more important than answers. Finding the right questions. I charmed him once by telling him that when I was a kid of nine or ten— precocious as hell—I made a big hit with my teachers at school and even the principal by suggesting that instead of us kids answering a lot of questions, the test should be us making up lists of questions." Shanti laughed lightly, a kind of gurgle in her throat. "So here I am trying to make up a list of the right questions. Is Cordelia my daughter? What's the difference, really? I know many adoptive parents and children who are as close as any family could ever be. Who is this Stella? Well, Jesus Christ, man! Pull yourself together! She's an actress who was found and engaged because she looks like you. So what?"

I went on and *on* until I heard Shanti say, "Thank you, Alan."

My time was up.

Finally, a letter from Cordelia.

Dear Daddy,

Sorry about not writing sooner or oftener but you have no idea how complicated life has been. The main thing I have to tell you is that I have never been happier in all my life! I am content and relaxed and occupied and confident that I am doing the really right thing. So please be happy for me and with me.

Tim turned up and I saw him several times—four to be exact. Surprisingly pleasant times they were, too. No scrapping, no bitterness, a few laughs even. I suppose that my improved mental condition contributed a lot. I really was a fish out of water up there in that business. I told Tim something I can tell you now in a letter which I could never have dreamed of telling you in person: I really hate the theater and everything about it. On both sides of the footlights. (I know there are no foots in Stratford but you know what I mean!) It seems to me—and always has—a silly game, all that pretending. And Shakespeare, in my opinion, is the worst. Sure, if you spend time studying the folios and footnotes and commentaries and variorums and all, you get a rough idea of what he is getting at. But most of it to most audiences is pure gobbledegook, and you know it.

Tim told me that when he was at Yale Drama they did a production of *Twelfth Night* as close as they could to the way it was done in Shakespeare's time. They constructed a rough replica of the Globe Theater—the size of two tennis courts, he said. The audience mostly standing, in what they called the pit, out of doors. Fruit and pastry and mead sellers going about. The female parts played by boys and the text spoken in Elizabethan rather than modern British speech. He said it sounded entirely different (and even more obscure I'll bet!).

By the way, I used to feel guilty and inferior about my inability to appreciate or even understand Shakespeare, until I heard that my beloved W. S. Gilbert was a confirmed Shakespeare hater. There's a lovely anecdote about him. Want to hear it? Okay. He once said to a friend, "Shakespeare's too obscure. Now, what does this mean? 'I would as lief be thrust through a quicket hedge as cry pooh to a callow throstle.'" And the friend said, "Simple. A man who loves songbirds would prefer to make his way through a thorny hedge rather than disturb one. But I don't recall the line. What play is it from?" "No play," said Gilbert. "I just made it up—and damned good Shakespeare it is!" Like it?

And as far as my ever being a part of the theater and learning lines and trying to be convincing and wooing the audience—it was never my thing, but always embarrassing. Now, Daddy, this is not to say that I don't admire you and your dedication and your success—I'm speaking only for myself. No doubt you think what *I'm* doing is silly—so there we are. Let's at least try to respect each other's aims and aspirations and values. Okay?

This will kill you! It almost killed *me!* I expected Tim, when he came down here, to do a big pitch about us getting married and me coming back to the company but he surprised the hell out of me by suggesting only the first part. I then pointed out how impractical—in fact, impossible—it would be, but he didn't agree at all. He saw nothing incompatible about our two diverse careers. Plus which, he said he had changed his mind completely—that our adventure had changed his mind completely—about children and that he was ready to start one on the spot! I declined this kind invitation. All this was on our first meeting. I have to confess that I didn't trust him for a minute—I could sense a trap—in fact, since I seem to have loosened up to this degree, I may as well tell you that I thought you and Mom were somehow behind it! Forgive me. Anyway by the third evening—now, get this—he said he would give up the theater and come here to school with me and later on we could pursue a joint career as veterinarians! Have you ever heard of anything so asinine? It didn't take me long to convince him that he had no more chance of succeeding in it than I ever would have had in the theater—but he really impressed me. Anyway, we parted as friends and he urged me to "keep thinking it over," which I'm afraid I'm going to have no time for. I told him I would probably wind up marrying a horse! It was a joke, but he didn't laugh.

I have had a few postcards from our world travellers. They seem to be enjoying themselves—but I will bet (a silk pajama!) not half as much as I am.

That's all for now—I am on my way to Urine Analysis (Elementary), you'll be thrilled to know, I'm sure.

    Cordelia (Standish, not Lear)

Lunch with Rusty Schneider at the Athletic Club. "She left Birmingham in nineteen fifty-eight," he informed me, "and returned in sixty-two—but up to now we can't seem to find out where she was."
"Wouldn't her passport have that information?"
He regarded me in the way that a professional always regards an amateur.

"Yes, sir, it would—or should—but it doesn't."

"Why not?"

"It's the first fishy note that's turned up."

"What is?"

"Some business about a lost passport. The new one, of course, has only the record of her most recent trips—England to Canada to here."

"I don't see that that's so fishy. I once lost my passport."

"*Did* you?" he said. "Well, there you are."

"Anything else?"

"Yes, I have a copy of Stella's birth certificate. Expensive."

"May I see it?"

"Sure."

He handed me a blurred gray copy. My eye picked out: Smith, Stella; female; 26 February 1962; Mother: Tobitt, Bridget Margaret; Father: unknown.

"May I keep this?" I asked.

"Sure thing," he said. "You're paying for it."

Another devastating dream: I am married to Bridget, for God's sake. We are in the audience at Stratford. We have come to see our daughter, Stella, in *King Lear*. Bridget is brimming with happy excitement, telling everyone around us who I am and who Stella is, while the performance is in progress. It does not seem at all strange to me that I am simultaneously in the audience and on the stage.

CORDELIA?

I am playing Lear. A scene with Cordelia:

> STELLA *(as Cordelia)*
> *The quality of mercy is not strained*
> *It droppeth as the gentle rain from heaven.*

> I *(as Lear)*
> *You don't hold any mystery for me, darling,*
> *do you mind? There isn't a particle of you*
> *I don't know, remember, and want.*

Great. She is playing *The Merchant of Venice* and I am responding with *Private Lives*.

> STELLA
> *Then take thy bond, take thy pound of flesh.*

> I
> *Would you be young always if you could choose?*

> STELLA
> *No, I don't think so, not if it meant having awful bulls' glands popped into me.*

> I
> *Cows for you dear, bulls for me.*

> STELLA
> *But just a pound of flesh; if thou takest more—*

> I
> *Women should be struck regularly—like gongs!*

The curtain falls.

Clearly, I could not tell *that* one to Shanti. She'd have me committed.

"I saw Stella's birth certificate this afternoon," I said to Shanti. "Father unknown. I must say that gave me a little jolt. I don't know why, but it did. For some reason it got me to wondering if Mrs. Ponsonby really *is* her mother. She's a weird, mysterious woman. I wish I thought there was some way I could get her to open up. The only way to her would be career—I mean Stella's career. That Mrs. Ponsonby is by all odds the most ambitious human being I've ever encountered, and I've lived among ambitious people most of my life. If I could devise some way of convincing her that I could—I mean that I *would*—do something for Stella but that she'd have to tell me—oh, what the hell am I talking about? Look, Shanti, I may as well tell you the truth—that is to say, tell myself the truth. These sessions with you have been among the most interesting and valuable experiences I've ever known. And what makes it all the more remarkable is the fact that you've helped me without saying a word. How do you do it? What you've done is help me to help myself, I suppose. Is that it? And I think I feel close enough to you now so that tomorrow I'm going to tell you the thing I haven't been able to tell you—or anyone—up to now."

I took Mrs. Ponsonby and Stella out to dinner at Sardi's. They had never been there and were carried away by the theatrical atmosphere and the people they recognized, and who recognized me, thank God. Several pals stopped by the table—and every single one of them remarked on Stella's resemblance to me. In fact, after the third one it got to be a joke and the three of us laughed about it each time.

They were entertained by the wall caricatures and excited when they came on mine.

"It don't 'alf do you justice," said Mrs. Ponsonby. "You're 'andsomer than that by a long jump."

"Thank you, Mrs. Ponsonby."

"Don't you imagine the time 'as come for you to call me Bridget? That's my name, y'know."

She smiled coquettishly. Was she being flirtatious? I thought so.

"Very well, Bridget. Bridget it is."

"Done and done!" she said, and offered her glass to be clinked.

Ideas went racing through my head. What if I romanced her? Where would that get me? In trouble, I suppose.

They insisted that I order for them.

"After all, dearie, it's your place. If we were at the Ivy, I'd be only too 'appy to do the honors."

So I ordered. Antipasto, canelloni, endive and

watercress salad, boccone dolce. Valpolicello wine.

The hour was a success in every way except for the subject that hung over us: the Actors' Equity hearing on the following day.

"I think they'll get the idea," I said. "Put on your best look-alike makeup, Stella."

"I shall," she said.

"Oh, it'll be different than Canada," said Bridget. "Down 'ere she'll be the only foreigner in the company. Ain't that so?"

"Yes, but they've been known to be pretty sticky sometimes. The rule is that the foreign player has to be a star."

"Or *unique*," said Bridget. She quoted: "'—that the Actor whose services are sought will be providing unique services which cannot be performed by any current member of Equity and that there is no citizen of the United States or resident alien domiciled in the U.S. capable of performing such services—' *That's* the rule."

I was astonished.

"Where did you get all that?"

"Up at Equity. I asked for all the rules and regulations and all the gen and they gave it to me. I'm the girl's manager, aren't I? And that's managin'."

"It certainly is."

"Would you like me to manage *you?*" she asked, giggling.

"I'll think about it."

"Do."

CORDELIA?

"What beats me is, I've been a member of Actors' Equity for over twenty-eight years and I never knew that. I thought the rule was simply star."

"No, no, you're quite wrong."

"Well, hell," I said, brightening. "I don't see that we have a problem at all. Unique. What could be the more unique problem—or solution?"

Bridget looked across the room and squinted. "I *know* that gentleman," she said. "What's 'is name? D'y'know?"

"Which one?"

"There in the corner with the stout gentleman."

"Oh, yes. He's a producer. Frank Palmer."

"Of course!" she cried. "I *knew* I knew him. I used to see him in Palm Beach when—" She stopped abruptly, picked up her wineglass and sipped slowly. Her face was all at once flushed.

I looked at Stella, who was finding it difficult to contain her astonishment.

I said, "I thought you said you'd never been to the States before, Bridget."

"No, no. You misunderstood me. I said I'd never been to *New York City* before."

"Oh."

Something odd here. What?

After dinner I walked them home. They were still at the Wellington.

In the lobby, Stella said, "Thank you so much. It was smashing, truly smashing."

"Yes, it was," echoed Bridget.

Stella and I shook hands. Then she leaned over

and kissed my cheek. Bridget offered her hand and although she did not follow Stella's lead there was something interesting communicated by her fingers.

I phoned Rusty.

"She was in Palm Beach," I told him. "Probably during that unaccounted-for time. Nineteen fifty-eight to nineteen sixty-two."

"Thanks," he said. "That's a good lead. See, if she was in Palm Beach she was probably working, wouldn't you say?"

"I should think so."

"So she'd've had to have a work permit—a green card and so on. We'll check it out. It may take some time, this is the busy season down there."

"No good," I said. "I need the dope fast."

"We'll do our best, fella."

As I told all this to Shanti, it seemed minor and unimportant. I felt foolish.

"I suppose," I said, "by this time I strike you as a full-blown neurotic."

To my astonishment, she spoke. "What do you think the word 'neurotic' means?"

I looked up at her. "Was that *you?*" I asked. "Actually *speaking?*"

She laughed. "Yes, as I told you. My turn. What does the word mean to you?"

"Well, come to think of it, I'm not sure. I guess it

CORDELIA?

means looking at the dark side of everything—imagining that the worst is always going to happen—am I close? Unreasonably anxious and worried? Without sufficient or logical reason."

"Not bad," she said. "Not bad. Better than most. But muddy. Let me tell you how Dr. Freud himself described it. 'Suppose,' he once said, 'that a New York society lady has accompanied her husband on a hunting trip in Africa. They are camping in a tent in the jungle. In the middle of one night she wakes up her husband in terror and says, "I believe there is a snake slithering around under the bed." The husband looks, searches, finds nothing. "Go back to sleep," the husband says. "You're just neurotic." The husband is *absolutely wrong*. But if that same lady sleeping with the same husband on the nineteenth floor of their Fifth Avenue apartment, wakes him in the middle of the night and says, in terror, "I believe there is a snake slithering around under the bed," *now* the husband can call her neurotic and be absolutely *right*.'"

I thought about it for a minute then asked, "And how does that apply to me?"

"You have not, so far as I can see, imagined the impossible. Details, clues, happenings, circumstances have come up to trouble you. You are trying to bring them to light. You may be overwrought and perhaps too imaginative—after all, you are an artist—but neurotic, no, not so far as I can see."

"Will you withhold your judgment until I tell you the next part?"

"Most assuredly."

"First of all, I want to apologize. I should have told you this sooner. Maybe right away, but I couldn't."

"Go on."

I turned away from her and began. "Last winter . . . in Chicago . . . the . . . repressed . . . sexual feeling I had felt for my daughter Cordelia for some time surfaced and was expressed." I looked up and saw, thought I saw, that the contained, impassive, composed professional was shocked. Her dark skin seemed to change color to a sort of purple. Yes, I thought, red and brown would produce just that hue. Her black eyes seemed to widen and she took a deep breath. "Wait," I said. "I'm afraid I've given you a wrong impression here." I began to tremble and broke into a sweat. I stood up and a voice other than mine—perhaps another person—took over. "Don't look at me like that!" I shouted. "I didn't fuck her, for Christ's sake!"

"Calm yourself, Alan."

I tried to pour a glass of water from a nearby carafe on her desk but it shook in my hand and I spilled water all over her desk.

"Sorry," I said.

"No matter," she said, mopping up the mess I had made.

She poured a glass of water for me. I drank it all and sat down. I could not go on. There was a long pause and just as I was on the verge of getting up and leaving, Shanti said, quietly, "You didn't fuck her.

CORDELIA?

Go on."

She had got me back on the track. I was impressed, then thought, well, what the hell, that's her business. I went on.

"All right. I'm not saying that I didn't *want* to or that I don't want to right now. And what I don't understand, can't understand, is how this could have happened to me. I have two other daughters, both of them lovely and alluring. Comely—where the hell did that word come from?—they're knockouts, both of them, and we've always been free and easy with them, skinny-dipping in pools and on beaches, they're constantly piling into bed with us, usually for Sunday breakfast and all sorts of displays of affection and cuddling. But I noticed several times with Cordy, when she came on—good God Almighty! I just realized something ... this minute ... it's been out of my mind for years, probably because I put it out, but I remember now ... it's crystal clear ... several times when she hugged me, Cordy, kissed me, touched me ... it would happen. An erection. Yes, I'd forgotten that or blocked it out. Embarrassing as hell. Never with the others, only with her ... with Cordy. All right, now. Back to last winter—Jesus God, this is hard to do ..." I stopped again and waited, trying to collect my jumbled thoughts.

After a time, Shanti's voice: "Last winter?"

"I'd been coaching her. We'd learned a scene from *Romeo and Juliet*. We were in a room together, alone. Her room. The business of the scene had some kissing in it. I'd been trying to teach her to let go, follow instinct . . . she's not much of a natural actress, so . . . we played the scene and did one or two kisses and then . . . and then . . ." My mouth went dry. I needed water, got it, and continued. "How can I put it? The roof caved in. We kissed . . . really kissed . . . out of control. She thought, I'm sure she thought that it was all acting, but I knew . . . know . . . different. I wanted to strip her and mount her then and there, I don't deny it . . . that's what I wanted to do!" My heart was beating far too hard and fast.

"Why didn't you?" she asked quietly.

"Because I managed somehow to gain control of myself—and in any case, she was off to find her boyfriend . . . said the scene had excited her . . . the scene, the rehearsal . . . she had no idea it had been real."

"Alan," she said, "you are too hard on yourself."

I looked up at her.

"Oh!" she said quickly, and smiled an embarrassed smile.

Then *I* smiled, then we both laughed at the apt usage, the revealing pun she had used. The shared laugh broke the tension, thank God, and communication was again possible.

"We cannot be held responsible, Alan, for what we think nor for what we feel—only for what we *do* or *fail* to do. All of us think the most dreadful things—and the most wonderful. We often want to kill or maim. If I told you some of *my* sexual fantasies, you would be shocked. No, let us have a free flow of the process of imagination and then let us work toward civilizing ourselves and one another to bring about a livable society . . . Now, incestuous impulses are not uncommon, but for the most part, normal persons keep them in check—often sublimating them into other activities. Are you certain that what happened was not acting taking over—'let-go' as you call it?"

"I wish I could say yes, but the answer is no, and that's why I'm trying to convince myself that she's not my daughter. Oh, God! Even as I say it it sounds like the most lame cop-out imaginable, but that's what I'm working on, that's what I'm trying to prove."

"To whom?"

"To myself, of course."

"And suppose you should succeed in doing so, what then?"

"Well, then at least I'll know I'm not an incestuous monster."

"And then?"

"And then—why, and then I don't know."

"I would strongly advise you to consider both a positive and negative outcome, and a course of action for each."

"All right."

"Alan, need I remind you that you are an actor, and as such, capable of flights of imagination, as they say? Do you not find that you do a great deal of acting in life as well as in the theater? We all do, naturally—but players more than others."

"Look, Shanti, I have no illusions or delusions about my profession. I don't argue with those who maintain that actors are grown-up children. I may well be. I don't consider my work an intellectual pursuit by any means. Sure, I feel more than I think. I act and react more powerfully than most. Cordy's often said to me, 'Daddy, you're *too sensitive!*' I can just hear her. I suppose I am, and yet, I've got to get this thing out of my system one way or another, or go under."

"You're not going to go under, Alan. I can promise you that, at least."

"Thank you, Shanti. *Thank you.*"

Then the most terrifying dream of them all: I am with Cordy and Stella in that room of Cordy's at the Whitehall in Chicago. Both of them are sitting on the bed. I am in the armchair facing them, telling them the whole story. The truth of who they really are.

"So you're my daughter, Stella," I say. And turning to Cordy, "And you're not."

They look at each other. Cordy screams a single piercing scream that can doubtless be heard by all the world. Stella smiles serenely.

When Cordy stops screaming, I say to her, "So you see, it's perfectly all right for us to go to bed together." To Stella: "Would you leave now, please, so we can go to bed together?"

CORDELIA?

I look at Cordy who is holding my .45 automatic pistol. She aims it at Stella's head and fires. The room is filled with smoke. When it clears, they are sitting on the bed as before and I'm telling them the story again. The scene repeats, but at the end Cordy doesn't aim the pistol at Stella. She puts it to her own head and fires, creating a gory mess. The room is again filled with smoke, but this time the smoke is red.

It clears. The scene again. Cordy and her pistol. She comes steadily toward me, pointing it at me. I stand up and run backward. She fires.

I woke up, drenched. I got out of bed, threw off the wet pajamas and took a shower. As I changed into fresh pajamas, I remembered how my friend Guy Trosper died in his sleep. He dreamt that he was having a heart attack, woke up in terror, called Tony Baldwin, his doctor, and told him about it.

Tony laughed and said, "Take two aspirins and call me in the morning."

Guy said, "Please, Tony. Let me come over now."

"Don't be silly, Guy. Take a drink and go back to sleep."

Guy did and never woke up again.

I looked at the clock—5:00 A.M. I took off the fresh pajamas, put them away and got dressed. I went to the kitchen, made myself some coffee. While waiting for the water to boil, I ate a quart of caramel ice cream. Soon afterward, I sat drinking coffee and watching the early morning television programs.

Escape at last.

Twenty-Two

The hearing at Actors' Equity Association was not as bad as I had feared. The council members seemed far less hostile than the Canadians had been. Perhaps it was only because I felt more at home, at ease, and not foreign.

The usual questions, reexaminations of documents, a thorough, professional dissertation by Peter on his problems with the production. He told me later that he had written it out and committed it to memory.

"I am in full sympathy, ladies and gentlemen of the council, with the position of Actors' Equity Association. With over eighty-five percent of your membership unemployed, why indeed should you permit an outsider, so-called, or at least a non-member of your union to usurp a role that might be played by one of the unfortunate eighty-five percent? I can assure you that every effort has been made, for months past, to find a suitable American for this role who would fit the concept. Between Howard Feuer, Barry Moss and our own organization, we examined over two thousand photographs and resumes, interviewed four hundred and fifty-six actresses and auditioned a hundred and twelve, without success. As you know, a complication was caused when Cordelia Standish resigned for personal reasons. Now, *I* may be the one to blame. I may be the stubborn culprit who had the idea that for once it would be interesting and exciting and artful to have Lear and his daughters look like a family. Perhaps that idea was better in theory than in practice, but it worked, ladies and gentlemen. It worked beautifully, and I am not prepared to give it up. We are asking for a waiver of a single contract. We will have, including understudies and stage managers, thirty-seven *American* Equity contracts. How many Broadway productions offer that? I appeal to you, as theater professionals, to make a reasonable concession for the sake of art and of the theater. Thank you."

Damned if the council didn't applaud.

Then I spoke, less effectively.

Jay Barney, a member of the council, asked Stella. "Is it your intention, Miss Smith, to remain in America and pursue your career here?"

"No, sir," she said. "I believe my opportunities would be less limited at home, in England."

Good shot, I thought.

I prayed that no one would cue Bridget on and my prayer was answered.

The Kennedy man then got out impressive figures to show that there was no way this production could ever pay off—that it was strictly a prestige matter. For some reason, *he* seemed to impress them most. Everyone respects money, I suppose.

Much handshaking all around before we left.

Peter, Bridget, Stella and I repaired to Joe Allen's for a little victory celebration.

"Piece o'cake," said Bridget, "like I knew it *would* be."

"You were wonderful, Peter," said Stella. "Thank you."

He frowned. "You didn't think I got a little Billy Graham there for a minute?"

"I thought it was *all* Billy Graham," I said, "from beginning to end. What's wrong with that?"

"Well, anyway, Mrs. Ponsonby—" began Peter.

"Bridget . . ."

"Bridget, I think you can start looking for an apartment."

"—got one already," she said slyly. "Paid first and last month's rent. A sort of diddle sublet at Manhattan Plaza."

"But wasn't that taking a big chance, Bridget?" I asked. "How could you be so sure?"

"Because," she said, "I 'ave my reasons." She

smiled, but when she caught me looking at her, hard, the smile faded, and she added, "I prayed and lit a candle each and every day—at St. Patrick's, no less."

Another round of drinks.

Rusty Schneider came up to see me with a great deal of information.

"We own a wizard down there," he said. "Son of a bitch is about seventy-five years old. Used to be a New York detective, got retired, went to Florida, got antsy, and signed with us. He ought to be head of the F.B.I., this guy. Anyway. You were right. Bridget Ponsonby worked as a housemaid for the Schuyler family in Hobe Sound—that's right outside of Palm Beach and—"

"I *know* where it is," I snapped.

"Could I ask you, buddy, why do you always get hot when I tell you something you happen to know? I'm just doing the best I know here."

"Rusty, I apologize. You're right. I'm wrong. Put it down to nerves, O.K.?"

"Sure, no offense. Now, this next is gossip. Floyd says—"

"Who's Floyd?"

"Our Palm Beach guy."

"Oh."

"He says—now remember, this isn't fact, not information, just plain old-fashioned gossip. He says that this Schuyler kid, Tod—well, he's not a kid now, he was then. You know, polo player in Boca Raton, auto racer in Daytona—well, it seems he knocked her up, the maid, so there was a real buzz-buzz scandal, and of course, they made her get rid of it, and then they paid her off—handsomely, I gather, and then they threw her out. Gossip, remember, just gossip. A big item down there in Palm Beach at the time."

"Anything else?"

"Not today."

"Thanks, Rusty."

"I'll be calling."

I tried to put pieces of the jigsaw together. "Father unknown" on that birth certificate. "They made her get rid of it." But what if she didn't? Still nothing fits—this would have had to be a Palm Beach or a somewhere-in-America birth. No, not necessarily. She could have gone back to England and had the baby there.

I was nowhere.

The following afternoon we were informed by Willard Swire of Actors' Equity that the council had unanimously rejected our application.

"Those fuckers!" Bridget yelled when she heard the news. "Those filthy fuckers! What are we goin' to do?"

"Not much we *can* do," said Peter. "We have the right to appeal, but I'm afraid it's what's called an exercise in futility."

"Not at all," said Bridget, blazing. "Not at bloody all! I 'aven't 'ad *my* say yet."

I dreaded the next morning and tried in every way I knew to beg off, but the Kennedy man, our strongest card, had returned to Washington, and Peter said, "What the hell, there's nothing to lose. A couple of times they've reversed themselves, but usually when they were threatened with a cancellation of the whole production, and we're hardly in a position to do that."

Actors' Equity again. A spokeswoman explained that they were very sorry but that it was merely a question of precedent. The thin edge of the wedge, and so on.

"But what about the 'unique clause'?" I asked. "I didn't know about it myself until recently."

"That was taken into consideration," said another member of the council. "We feel that the word means something else. A special, irreplaceable ability, or physical characteristic."

"That's not what *my* dictionary tells me," I said.

A shrug was the response.

"Could we go to law on this, Willard?" asked Peter. "Shouldn't the law interpret that clause?"

"No," he replied. "It's *our* law, not the government's."

"Please," said Bridget, and I winced. God only knew what was coming now. "How can you be so cruel as to deprive my child of 'er first great opportunity? Look at these cuttings!" She went to the table and passed around Xerox copies of the Canadian notices. She began to cry. "You'll break 'er spirit, you will!" As the tears became copious, I became more embarrassed. "Isn't there one of you with an 'eart?" she cried. There was no response, other than abashment at this mewling performance—and performance indeed it turned out to be, because she stopped crying as abruptly as she had begun, stepped away from the table, pointed an accusing finger at the council and waved it slowly back and forth until she was sure that each member had been included. Then she said, "All right, you fuckers, now *you* listen to *me*—"

The chairman rapped his gavel sharply. "Sit down, Mrs. Ponsonby."

"*Bollocks* to you!"

"If you don't sit down and behave yourself, I'm going to adjourn."

"Do what y'like," she shot back, "but there's no *way* you're going to keep my girl out of this show. You can't."

"*Why* can't we?" asked the chairman.

Bridget drew herself up, took a deep breath, and said quietly, "Because she's an American *citizen!* That's why!"

"What!"

"Since when?"

"Since she was born here, you pouf!"

If Stella had not fainted and fallen out of her chair at this point, I honestly believe that I would have done so myself.

It took the better part of ten minutes to bring her around, then she asked to be excused. Peter went with her, and I was left to hear the details.

Bridget was calmer now. "My daughter Stella was born in Palm Beach, Florida on February twenty-six, nineteen hundred and sixty-two. 'Ere's 'er birth certificate. Name of father blank. I could fill it out for you but I am enjoined by this court order from doin' so. I put Smith on the certificate. She 'ad to 'ave a name, 'adn't she?" She produced still another document. "This is 'er first passport." As she handed it over, I caught a glimpse of the infant photo it bore. "She became Stella Ponsonby when I married Sam Ponsonby and 'e 'ad the goodness to adopt 'er legal." More papers. The council, along with us, was getting dizzy.

"Well," said Willard, "in the circumstances, we are certainly going to have to review and reconsider the entire matter. May we borrow these documents?"

"Of course not. I'll send you copies."

"We'll make them."

"I need no favors from the likes of you," she said, and gathered up her records.

"Is that all, then?" asked Willard, as though he could think of nothing better to say.

"No," said Bridget. "One more thing." She stepped back, took a stance, and in her fruity Cockney recited loudly:

CORDELIA?

Fuck 'em all
Big and small
They got no class
They can kiss my arse.
There was an old woman
Who lived in a shoe
And she can kiss
My fuckin' arse too!

She sailed out of the room in the manner of a duchess taking leave of her queen.

I was left alone with the council. We were silent for a time, then I said, "I'm planning to present her on Sunday nights in a one-woman show of Shakespeare's heroines. If you'll give me clearance."

The council members laughed harder than the lame joke warranted.

The four of us stood awkwardly on the sidewalk for a while. There seemed to be either nothing or too much to say.

"Are you all right, Stella?" I asked.

"I will be, thank you."

"She's all right," said Bridget.

"I'd like very much to meet with you as soon as possible, Bridget."

"Any time."

"I'll call you."

"Shall I get you a cab?" asked Peter.

"No," said Bridget, "we'll walk."

"I'd rather a cab, Mother."

"Come on," said Bridget, and they went off.

Peter and I went to Downey's and ordered doubles. I asked, "How close were you to bringing up the British passport we saw in Canada?"

"Tip of my tongue."

"It's bound to come up, isn't it?—when Canadian Equity gets wind of all this?"

"No matter. She apparently has dual citizenship, that's all. Two passports. My mother had two. Very convenient sometimes."

"Also convenient to have two birth certificates." I said. "Explain that one."

"I don't even want to try. We've got ourselves mixed up with a diddler par excellence here."

"I think she's someone to watch with the greatest care."

"Bonkers, maybe?"

"Maybe."

"What do you want to meet with her about?"

"Damned if I know," I lied. "It just seemed like the thing to say at that moment."

We sat in the living room of my apartment, drinks in hand. It was late, after eleven, but I had needed time to plan my attack.

"Bridget," I said, "I'm going to put it to you as

plainly as I can. I think Stella has a great future—in the theater, in films, whatever she wants. I can help her—she can probably do it without my help, but I could speed things up—"

"Oh, I know that, God bless y'!"

"Never mind the bullshit, Bridget. We're both operators, so let's level."

"I'm game."

"All right then, to begin with—where was Stella born?"

"In the United States."

"*Where* in the United States? Don't lie," I cautioned.

"Why would I lie?"

"Because you're a liar, that's why."

"I'm lookin' after me own," she said proudly.

"*Where* in the United States was she born?" I repeated.

"In Palm Beach."

"Where in Palm Beach?"

"In 'ospital."

"What hospital?"

A pause. Too long. "I don't remember the name of it."

"Come *on!*"

"I don't," she said, whining.

"Do you remember the name of her father?"

She paled, as she looked at me with some apprehension, or was it fear? "I'll *never* tell y' that. *Never.*"

"You don't need to, I know it."

"Ha!" she scoffed.

"Tod Schuyler," I said. "Ring a bell?"

"You bastard!" she shouted as she leaped from the chair and dropped her glass. "What's it to *you?* You've got it wrong anyway."

"No, I haven't. I have not got it wrong. I've got it right. Tod Schuyler. And what's it to me? Nothing. I merely want you to know that I know a good deal about you, and I'm striking a bargain with you. You tell me what I want to know and I'll help Stella. *More* than help. I promise you that I'll see her right to the top. But you have to open up with me, Bridget."

"And what if I don't?" she asked defiantly.

"If you don't, and I mean right now, tonight— she's out of the company. As of now."

She sat down heavily. "You wouldn't!"

"You bet your ass—I mean arse—I would."

"Why? Why would you?"

"Because I don't like to be diddled, or kidded or lied to—especially about someone I'm about to accept as a protegée." I decided to try a softer tack. I moved to her and continued quietly. "You can trust me, Bridget—whatever's said here tonight is between us alone. It doesn't include my wife, or Stella. Just you and me."

"Do y' swear it?"

"I do."

"All right." Her voice took on a new coloration, and she began to speak in a dreamy faraway tone. "Tod Schuyler. Yes. Tod. I was one of the upstairs maids. He 'ad 'em all, but then when 'e got me in the family way, I 'ad to tell 'im, didn't I? I was twenty-two years old. I 'ardly knew anythin' about anythin', but I knew I was in trouble, serious trouble. The father wasn't too bad, but that *Mrs.* Schuyler, she was a gorgon for fair. They were all rich, don't y'know, and 'ad all kinds of pull—politicians and all. The ol' biddy told me I'd 'ave to go and take care of it, but it's against my religion, and I refused." She stopped for a moment, looked at me and said, "The name of the hospital was St. John's."

I fixed her another drink as she went on.

"Oh, there were all kinds of threats. I was out of the 'ouse by then—in a motel. Tod gave me some money. But she kept callin'. I think she was 'avin' me watched and followed, and once she said, 'All right, go ahead and 'ave it, but then we'll take it. You're in no position to bring up a child.' And I thought they *might* get it away from me somehow. So I decided to go and 'ave the operation then, but before I did I went to see Father Michael. I 'ad to. Oh, he's a sainted man, and I told him I 'ad to go ahead, that I 'ad to. He said there were places would help me. He told me that in New York at the Foundlin' 'ospital they 'ad a whole arrangement for unwed mothers and that he'd find out about it for me. But I was still scared about what they might do, so a few days after Stella was born, I got a taxi and I moved to Miami without tellin' anyone, not even Father Michael. And by then I knew that I 'ad to get back to England, so I got the baby a passport and made my plane reservations and flew to New York."

At this point in her recital—as she spoke the words "New York"—my skin began to crawl. My brain began to swim. I wanted to hear the rest of it quickly, *right now*. I also did not want to hear it at all. I tried to make myself leave the room, ordered myself out, but I could not move. She was still going on.

". . . about forty-five minutes on the plane when the baby took real bad, took very ill with a burnin' fever and the stewardesses, they were frightened and they 'ad the captain radio for an ambulance to be waitin' and it was, and I got her right into 'ospital."

I could not ask the next question, but I had to.

"What hospital?"

Before she could answer, I went deaf. She went on talking and I could see her but I could not hear a word. I wanted to say, Wait! I can't hear you, but I had gone not only deaf but dumb as well. My thoughts were racing, my mind receiving in spite of myself . . . same hospital? Same time? Where is Tod Schuyler? If I could find him, would Cordelia look like *him?* Is he alive? Where?

". . . but it wasn't till the third day that 'e said she was out of danger. I called Father Michael and thanked him for his prayers. Then 'e came up—on his own—to be with me, and I could tell the whole time 'e was worried. But then, when the doctor told us that Stella was goin' to be all right, 'e was *still* worried. So finally I asked 'im why, and 'e took me downstairs, into the chapel and—"

CORDELIA?

Was *he* still around? This Father Michael? Could I check some of this with *him?* Was she telling the truth? Was I going nuts? How much of this should I tell to Shanti? To Rusty? To Pam . . . ?

". . . so I said, 'But 'ow *could* they do that? What right 'ave they got? Wouldn't the law protect me?' And Father Michael said, 'Bridget, the law don't mean what *you* think it means, and it don't mean what *I* think it means. It means what the judge *says* it means.' 'And do they own all the judges?' I asked 'im. And he said, 'No, not *all.*' So then I knew why 'e was so worried, and I begged 'im to tell me what to do, and 'e said, 'I can't. I know what you *should* do, what *I'd* do in your place, but I can't tell you. I can't advise you. You do understand my position, don't you?' And 'e went on talkin' like this for a long time, and after a while I began to see what was 'appenin'. 'e was tellin' me what to do without tellin' me. 'e was tellin' me to get my baby out of there before it was too late. Finally I said, 'Yes, Father, I see. I know. Yes. But how?' And 'e said . . ."

I found myself standing in silence again, a drink in either hand. Was I dreaming one of my terrifying dreams? Could all this, could *any* of this be true? *Should* I tell Pam? Ask Pam? Don't be ridiculous. Ben? Of course not. But I can't carry this alone, goddam it . . .

". . . so we sat there in the coffee shop for about 'alf an 'our, and 'e kept lookin' at the different nurses comin' in and goin' out, but it didn't get through to me what 'e was thinkin'. Finally 'e got up and went over to one of the nurses and started talkin' to 'er. 'e talked to 'er for a long time and kept lookin' over at me. It was as though they were talkin' about *me,* and then all of a sudden I got the idea of what 'e was sayin' without sayin'. That . . ."

What *was* he saying, for the love of God? That she should spirit the baby away? Take it, steal it? Well, hardly stealing since it was her own child. But what is all this nurse stuff? Oh. He was advising her to dress as a nurse and do it that way, was he? Would a priest do that?

". . . to Bloomin'dale's and bought the outfit and 'ad it ready—but I was too scared to go there with it and maybe I wouldn't 'ave if I 'adn't gone back to the 'ospital and out in front I saw that Rolls-Royce station wagon with Florida license plates and I knew I was done for and I rushed 'ome and put on the nurse's uniform—white stockings, shoes, the lot— and I went back to the 'ospital and the station wagon was still there. I didn't wait for any lift. I ran up the stairs. I 'ad this big shoppin' bag with me. I went into the nursery and waited till I was the only one there. Then I put Stella into the shoppin' bag and went on out and out and down and down—"

How did you know it was Stella? I almost asked, but checked myself. It didn't take too much imagination to figure it . . . she didn't check, she grabbed up the infant under "Smith," she *thought.* Except in her rush it was the one under "Standish," obviously right next to it. Alphabetical. Jesus . . . So I had the story, finally. Decide what to do with it later.

"... but Father Michael was waitin' there for me. He'd rented a car—said it was safer than a taxi or an 'ired car. No trouble at the airport, especially seein' as 'ow I was with 'im—with a priest and an infant—they greased the way for me. I want a drink."

As I got another whiskey for her, more questions poured into my head but I realized that absolute silence was my only weapon now. There would be time to sort it all out later. I handed her the drink.

"And that's the God's truth," she said. "I swear it by the Father and the Son and the 'oly Ghost."

"I believe you," I said. "Go home now. I'm tired."

She finished her drink in a gulp, started out, came back, grasped my hand and kissed it. "You're my friend," she said. "And you can *'ave* Stella."

She had been gone for half an hour before the full implication of her remark hit me.

Twenty-Three

I still can't explain how I ever got through rehearsals. The irony of my suspicion that Cordy was the issue of Pam's infidelity didn't escape me. Blue eyes ... Cordy looking more like Pam than me ... both being less than natural, instinctive actors ... all innocent coincidences blown out of proportion by me ... I was right, more right than I dared believe, but not for the reasons I thought. Cordy was *not* my child, but she was not Pam's child either ... Stella ...

I talked to Stella often, and she seemed to want to talk to me.

"I don't know what my mother could have been thinking of," she said one day. "All that flummery just to keep it secret from me, that I'm illegitimate? Who cares, anyway? And she must have known I'd be bound to find out in time. I do apologize. I know it was most embarrassing for you and for Peter."

"No, no," I said. "My father used to say, 'We can choose our friends but our relatives are wished on us.'"

"She's a good sort, really. Means well."

"I know."

"And done everything for me, God knows."

Was this my daughter I was talking to? My flesh and blood? Was it? Could it be?

On our first Sunday off, Shanti agreed to see me for a final session.

"It's more to thank you than anything else," I said.

"Not at all."

"I doubt I could have gotten through this without your guidance. It really was a sickness of some kind. I'm at peace, now except for worrying about the play. By the way, will you and your husband come to the opening of our play as my guests?"

"We should be honored."

"I hope, Shanti, that I never find myself in a bind of any kind again, but if I do . . . thank God I know where to come."

"I'll be here when you need me. If."

"You think I will?"

"Possibly. Probably. But I hope you have learned from all this to trust your own ability to handle such situations. If that is so, I have done my job. If not, you will need more therapy . . . You look tired.

CORDELIA?

Too tired."

"Maybe because I am tired, too tired. Could that be the reason?"

"But I *am* happy for you," she said.

I wondered if I had taken her in? I couldn't tell from that inscrutable mask. We shook hands professionally.

"Goodbye, Alan."

"Thank you, Shanti."

On the following Sunday, a final meeting with Rusty and Archie.

"I'm sorry it was so costly," said Archie. "But it was the speed you insisted on. If we'd had more time, it would've been less."

"No complaints," I said. "I found out everything I wanted to know."

Rusty spoke. "Boy, that Floyd down there . . . once he gets started you can't stop him. Look at this." He handed me a document from which I learned that the senior Schuylers were deceased; she, in 1971 of a stroke; he, in 1973, a suicide. Tod Schuyler and three young women were killed when his Lear jet crashed near Palm Springs in 1970. (Lear! I hope *my* Lear doesn't crash!) An investigation proved that all four had ingested cocaine.

Further on I read, "And that oddball Father Michael O'Greely you asked about left the priesthood in 1967, converted to Buddhism and is said to be at present in a monastery somewhere in Utah. Can check it if you want."

"So on that priest," said Rusty. "Would you like

Floyd to—"

"No, no," I said. "It's over."

Pam and Lynn returned from abroad. Why did they seem to be different people?

Twenty-Four

Opening night.

It was upon us all at once. Peter, kind and thoughtful, had had ten days of rehearsal with the new members of the company and understudies to keep the rest of us from getting stale. So Pam and the girls and Tim and Stella rehearsed only two weeks. It was enough.

I was, needless to say, preoccupied throughout rehearsals. My Stratford performance surfaced and I was able to get through the time somehow, but my thoughts and my concentration were, of course, elsewhere. Now that I knew, I didn't know what to do. Insofar as possible, I tried to put it out of my mind until after the opening. I *had* to. Time enough to deal with it then. How? Never mind. Later, later, later.

Why did it wait to strike me until the curtain was up and the performance underway? Why? Why did it stay below the surface until I sat in the glare of that most powerful of spotlights—the one generated by a thousand pair of eyes all looking at the same player?

The curtain had been up for no more than a minute and a half when, accompanied by my daughters and my entourage, I made my entrance. A splendid reception, and we were off.

Peter insisted that the first scene of the play be taken at a swift clip. He pointed out that the expository material is not very interesting and that many people are afraid of Shakespeare, so if you start with a lively tempo, they're somehow comforted. Lastly, speed tells the audience that the players are confident, and that relaxes them too. So, following his direction, I took off in high and felt I was going well until I came to the lines:

We have this hour a constant will to publish
Our daughters' several dowers, that further
  strife
May be prevented now.

That was when it hit me. I looked about and saw my three daughters together: Lynn, Laurette *and* Stella, and I went blank. The five seconds it took me to recover seemed like five minutes to the company and like half an hour to me—but I managed to recover and go on, in a considerable sweat.

All continued to go well. Regan expressed her

CORDELIA?

love. Then Goneril, in turn, and we were into the important Cordelia scene. She could not find it within herself to be as fulsome as her sisters.

Stella (as Cordelia) said:

*Unhappy that I am, I cannot heave
My heart into my mouth. I love your Majesty
According to my bond, no more nor less.*

It was without a doubt the purest, dearest reading of those lines I had ever heard, and I found it difficult to respond:

*How, how, Cordelia? Mend your speech a little
Lest you may mar your fortunes.*

It was during her next speech, delivered with her extraordinarily beautiful eyes on mine that I became undone:

*Good my Lord
You have begot me, bred me, loved me, I
Return those duties back as are right fit,
Obey you, love you, and most honor you.*

I heard no more for a time because with these lines she had inadvertently made my decision for me. Of course, I would not bury the truth. She was my daughter and life—lives—would have to be arranged or rearranged somehow into a new mold. I felt myself take the deepest breath I have ever inhaled just as my cue came. Relaxation was complete, and I went on to give the best performance of *Lear* I had ever given—modesty be damned— maybe the best performance *anyone* has ever given.

One of those nights. A real—not phony—ovation. Cheers. I felt like cheering myself.

The backstage crush. We received on the stage, we had to. Photographers. Radio microphones. Television cameras. Happy bedlam.

Faces. Shanti, with her husband, looking glamorous and exotic.

Darling Ben, who said, "I hate crowds. People are always stepping on me. See you at the party."

Cordy, with a bumpkin beau, kissing me and crying and saying extravagant things. I hugged her and thought, She's my daughter *too!*

Rusty, with a beautiful young blond boy (!); Archie, with an attractive woman I took to be his wife.

I wanted to get it over with and get to the Players Club, where Peter had planned a grand and elaborate party. There was to be a champagne supper, an entertainment on the stage, followed by dancing.

"What the hell?" he had said. "How often does one know that one has something to celebrate for certain? As a rule, all first-night parties are disastrous; merriment for an hour or so and then the radio and telly and reports of the press reviews come in and the party's over. But in this case, we know we're home free even if the New York boys who raved about the Stratford production say this is less good—and they might, you know, they might, the impact of the first time, you know—it won't make much difference. And anyway only a dunderhead could think that one was better. This company is magic, absolute magic."

So, the party. Peter had wisely restricted the number of invitations, so the club, although full, was not uncomfortably crowded. The food, supervised by Peter—a devoted gourmet and cuisine expert—was outstanding. The wines were choice. Flowers. Music, lighting. You either know how to give a party or you don't.

The program began with eight members of our company singing a rollicking version of Cole Porter's, "Another Op'nin, Another Show" from *Kiss Me, Kate*. I was surprised at the quality of the singing which had been coached by and was accompanied by John Kander.

Next, Peter, who was acting as the master of ceremonies, came on with a large tape recorder and played three radio reviews which he had taped earlier. All excellent for all. Applause. I looked over at Ben, who winked merrily. Should I tell him first?

The next number was a complete surprise. Peter

had gone over the program with me but had left this item out.

Laurette, Lynn and Cordy—in the costumes of Regan, Goneril and Cordelia—came tripping onto the stage. The introductory music that John was playing sounded familiar but it was not until they began that I recognized "Three Little Maids From School Are We" from *The Mikado* which had long been a party specialty of theirs. But performed in those costumes from *Lear* it became something else. I saw only Cordy. How would she react? What would she say, do? The number ended. They scored decisively.

Peter again. The curtain parted and there on the stage was a giant television screen. The lights went down and on came the five TV reviews: NBC, Channel 11, ABC, Channel 5, CBS. He had videotaped them an hour or so earlier. NBC was bad, very bad. So Peter opened with it, then repeated little pieces of it after each of the others—which were all raves.

Pam came on next in her jester's costume, sang a parody of "What Kind of Fool Am I?" and brought down the house. Pam, I thought, who had lavished nineteen years of devotion and worry and love on the wrong child.

Then John played—and his partner Fred Ebb performed—several numbers from various musicalized Shakespeare productions, *Swingin' the Dream, The Hot Mikado* and *West Side Story.*

Next Lynn and her partner Marcel danced the *pas*

de deux from the *Romeo and Juliet* ballet—beautifully. I kept praying he wouldn't drop her again.

Peter said, "And now, to prove that the performance tonight was not a fluke and that he can do it whenever he wishes, we present Mr. Alan Standish as King Lear."

Another surprise. It was Stella in my costume and wig and makeup doing a most terrifyingly accurate imitation of me in the "Blow, winds" scene. Voice, gestures, posture, expression, mannerisms (good and bad). She *was* me. I felt faint. At the end, a music cue and all at once she was singing in her own voice "Brush Up Your Shakespeare" from *Kiss Me, Kate* as the rest of the players on the program drifted on and joined her for the finale. I saw Stella and Cordy, standing beside each other, holding hands. The room was going round.

The party went on until 2:00 A.M. I danced with Pam, with Cordy, with Stella, Lynn, Laurette. They were all the same person. I got well plastered and do not remember much about the last hour—except vaguely—talking to Shanti, and Rusty, and Ben, who was full of praise. I remember *that* all right.

Also, I recall wandering into the kitchen looking for Peter to thank him for the event. I found him there arranging great baskets of hard-boiled eggs on which were painted Lear's head and which were going to be served at 1:00 A.M.

"I've got a great idea," I said.

"What's that?"

"Let's do *Lear* up in Stratford next summer. You play Lear and your three daughters play your three daughters."

"I haven't got three daughters."

"Are you sure?" I asked.

"Frankly, no. But listen, I wasn't going to mention this until next week, but as long as you've brought it up—I *know* what we're going to do at Stratford next year."

"What?"

"*Hamlet*. You and Pam as the Queen Mum and can you imagine what a wonderful Ophelia we're going to get from Stella?"

I said, "How about Pam as Hamlet—or Pamlet as Ham, and *I'll* play the Queen Mum, and they can both, the two of them, play Ophelia, too?"

"What?" he said, understandably confused.

"Don't be goofy," I said. "I'm too old for Hamlet by twenty years."

"Have you gone round the bend?" he shouted. "Age doesn't matter in the classics."

"Oh, is that a classic?"

"One of the great American Hamlets, Walter Hampden—he was the president of this club—he played Hamlet when he was fifty-five. Edwin Booth, for Christ's sake, whose *house* this is, played it at forty-seven. Garrick, fifty-nine. Forbes-Robertson —the greatest, I suppose—played it until he was *sixty!*"

"I know, but that was way back in the—"

"Barrymore, forty. Redgrave, fifty."

"You sound like a sports score. Redgrave wins by ten points!"

"Can I tell you something I know?" said Peter. "Not something I think, something I *know?*"

"What?"

"We're going to *do* it."

I thought, me as Hamlet, my wife as my mother, my daughter as my love! If I live through that one I'll live forever.

But I said nothing. We stood there looking at each other while he peeled two hard-boiled eggs, one for himself and one for me. We ate them in silence.

I said, "To pee or not to pee, that is the question," and went downstairs to the men's room.

I do *not* recall the trip home or getting to bed, but I slept until noon.

Pam woke me up with coffee and the papers.

"Good morning, *triomphateur,*" she said. So I knew all was well.

Twenty-Five

Now, how to go about the revelation?

I felt surprisingly fine in spite of the night before. Amazing what therapy there is in success.

I said to Pam, "I think I'd better get down to the club and sweat out, swim out, massage out this hangover if I'm going to play tonight."

"Do that," she said. "I'm going to bed."

In the steam room, I tried to form a plan of action. Who to tell first? Pam of course. We'd go on with it together. It would be a massive relief to have someone to share this with. And who next? Bridget, I suppose. Then, and only then, Cordy, and Stella. What would be the wisest course? Tell them together or separately? Together. No. Separately.

Was I going too fast? Were there legalities involved? Should I discuss it first with a lawyer? Which one? A stranger.

How was the mistake made at the hospital? I've already gone through that . . . Bridget, overwrought and terrified, must have erred, but maybe the hospital did it, mixed up the babies in their cribs . . . like they do lab reports and God knows what all . . . the hospital authorities could be questioned, a lawsuit of some sort be instituted? Negligence proved? Questions questions and more questions.

I moved into the dry-heat room, sat and sweated and thought. How would Pam react? Shock. And then? Disbelief. And when all had been proven, then what? Dismay, confusion. Had the nineteen years been a waste? No, of course not. A mistake, that's all, never mind how it happened. It happened.

Bridget? Her whole life was bound up in Stella, in Stella's talent and career. Now she would have a veterinarian for a daughter. She would almost surely dislike Cordy. What would Cordy make of *her?* What would she do? Where would she live? In England? In Texas? We would have to continue to look after her, of course—well, not *have* to, *want* to.

The publicity. What a story for the sensational press, or for any press for that matter. I could see the headlines now in the *Star,* in the *National Enquirer.* And what about the British press?

CORDELIA?

As I dove into the pool my head began to clear and I knew that it was time to consider what I had been avoiding and postponing for days, the effect on Cordy and Stella . . . Cordy learns that she is the illegitimate child of a wastrel and a housemaid. All at once she has no real father, and there is Bridget to deal with for the rest of her life. Stella. She has made peace with her situation, has some sort of living arrangement with Bridget, a career to pursue. Would she much care? Would she think the whole situation comical? Possibly.

On the massage table I found myself strangely relaxed as the excellent Victor worked. I went over the whole mess again in my mind. Which one of us would be better off afterward? Which one's worse? What would the upheaval accomplish? Without revealing anything to anyone, there was no reason why I could not look after Stella always. She would be, ostensibly, a protegée and a friend.

Life is complicated and chaotic enough. Why complicate it more?

"No!" I shouted, startling Victor, the masseur.

He stopped and asked, "What's a matter?"

I had made a decision. No, I would *not* tell Pam. No. Or Bridget. No. Or Cordy. No. Or Stella. No. I would keep it to myself. For the moment I felt great. And right. And even intelligent, which is something I don't feel too often.

I smiled contentedly and drifted off to sleep under Victor's rhythmic hands, thinking of next year's production of *Hamlet,* which would surely top this year's *Lear* . . .

A soaring second night performance. Unusual. They are traditionally something of a letdown. Then a sleepless night during which all my self-assurance evaporated and I convinced myself that I had made the wrong decision. After all, don't people have a right to know who they are, who their real parents are? Don't their parents have a right to know too? . . . Pam, Bridget, Stella, Cordy . . .

And so it went, day after ambivalent day until I was sick again.

Then, on the first Sunday, I told Pam some cock-and-bull about needing some important and personal medical advice, and flew out to Cincinnati to see Ben. But, as I've said, when I got there I found that I just couldn't tell him. I could only reveal that I was living with a killing problem. Without knowing what it was, how could he help? The wise advice he gave me was to write it down, write it out. And so I have.

My decision is made, finally, firmly. I shall tell no one, not ever.

Am I wrong?

ZEBRA BRINGS YOU EXCITING BESTSELLERS
by Lewis Orde

MUNICH 10 (1300, $3.95)

They've killed her lover, and they've kidnapped her son. Now the world-famous actress is swept into a maelstrom of international intrigue and bone-chilling suspense — and the only man who can help her pursue her enemies is a complete stranger . . . .

HERITAGE (1100, $3.75)

Beautiful innocent Leah and her two brothers were forced by the holocaust to flee their parents' home. A courageous immigrant family, each battled for love, power and their very lifeline — their HERITAGE.

THE LION'S WAY (900, $3.75)

An all-consuming saga that spans four generations in the life of troubled and talented David, who struggles to rise above his immigrant heritage and rise to a world of glamour, fame and success!

Available wherever paperbacks are sold, or order direct from the Publisher. Send cover price plus 50¢ per copy for mailing and handling to Zebra Books, 475 Park Avenue South, New York, N.Y. 10016. DO NOT SEND CASH.

ROMANCE AT ITS BEST . . .

LOVE ME WITH FURY (1248, $3.75)
by Janelle Taylor
When Alexandria discovered the dark-haired stranger who watched her swim, she was outraged by his intrusion. But when she felt his tingling caresses and tasted his intoxicating kisses, she could no longer resist drowning in the waves of sweet sensuality.

BELOVED SCOUNDREL (1259, $3.75)
by Penelope Neri
Denying what her body admitted, Christianne vowed to take revenge against the arrogant seaman who'd tormented her with his passionate caresses. Even if it meant never again savoring his exquisite kisses, she vowed to get even with her one and only BELOVED SCOUNDREL!

TIDES OF RAPTURE (1245, $3.75)
by Elizabeth Fritch
When honey-haired Mandy encounters a handsome Yankee major, she's enchanted by the fires of passion in his eyes, bewitched by the stolen moments in his arms, and determined not to betray her loyalties! But this Yankee rogue has other things in mind!

PASSION'S GLORY (1227, $3.50)
Each time Nicole looked into Kane's piercing dark eyes, she remembered his cold-hearted reputation and prayed that he wouldn't betray her love. She wanted faithfulness, love and forever—but all he could give her was a moment of PASSION'S GLORY.

Available wherever paperbacks are sold, or order direct from the Publisher. Send cover price plus 50¢ per copy for mailing and handling to Zebra Books, 475 Park Avenue South, New York, N.Y. 10016. DO NOT SEND CASH.

THE BEST IN HISTORICAL ROMANCE
by Sylvie F. Sommerfield

CHERISH ME, EMBRACE ME (1199, $3.75)

Lovely, raven-haired Abby vowed she'd never let a Yankee run her plantation or her life. But once she felt the exquisite ecstasy of Alexander's demanding lips, she desired only him!

SAVAGE RAPTURE (1085, $3.50)

Beautiful Snow Blossom waited years for the return of Cade, the handsome halfbreed who had made her a prisoner of his passion. And when Cade finally rides back into the Cheyenne camp, she vows to make him a captive of her heart!

REBEL PRIDE (1084, $3.25)

The Jemmisons and the Forresters were happy to wed their children —and by doing so, unite their plantations. But Holly Jemmison's heart cries out for the roguish Adam Gilcrest. She dare not defy her family; does she dare defy her heart?

TAMARA'S ECSTASY (998, $3.50)

Tamara knew it was foolish to give her heart to a sailor. But she was a victim of her own desire. Lost in a sea of passion, she ached for his magic touch—and would do anything for it!

DEANNA'S DESIRE (906, $3.50)

Amidst the storm of the American Revolution, Matt and Deanna meet—and fall in love. And bound by passion, they risk everything to keep that love alive!

Available wherever paperbacks are sold, or order direct from the Publisher. Send cover price plus 50¢ per copy for mailing and handling to Zebra Books, 475 Park Avenue South, New York, N.Y. 10016. DO NOT SEND CASH.

EXCITING BESTSELLERS FROM ZEBRA

STORM TIDE (1230, $3.75)
by Patricia Rae
In a time when it was unladylike to desire one man, defiant, flame-haired Elizabeth desired two! And while she longed to be held in the strong arms of a handsome sea captain, she yearned for the status and wealth that only the genteel doctor could provide—leaving her hopelessly torn amidst passion's raging STORM TIDE....

PASSION'S REIGN (1177, $3.95)
by Karen Harper
Golden-haired Mary Bullen was wealthy, lovely and refined—and lusty King Henry VIII's prize gem! But her passion for the handsome Lord William Stafford put her at odds with the Royal Court. Mary and Stafford lived by a lovers' vow: one day they would be ruled by only the crown of PASSION'S REIGN.

HEIRLOOM (1200, $3.95)
by Eleanora Brownleigh
The surge of desire Thea felt for Charles was powerful enough to convince her that, even though they were strangers and their marriage was a fake, fate was playing a most subtle trick on them both: Were they on a mission for President Teddy Roosevelt—or on a crusade to realize their own passionate desire?

LOVESTONE (1202, $3.50)
by Deanna James
After just one night of torrid passion and tender need, the dark-haired, rugged lord could not deny that Moira, with her precious beauty, was born to be a princess. But how could he grant her freedom when he himself was a prisoner of her love?

Available wherever paperbacks are sold, or order direct from the Publisher. Send cover price plus 50¢ per copy for mailing and handling to Zebra Books, 475 Park Avenue South, New York, N.Y. 10016. DO NOT SEND CASH.